SLUGGER

Stories that hit you in the mouth

Vol. 2

Edited by Sam Logan & Arwyn Sherman

Cover Art by Kae Ranck

Interior Layout & Format by Leo Otherland

Editors' Note

We're going to give it to you straight—there's some weird, creepy shit in here.

This second volume includes 10 original stories from another eclectic mix of horror-blending subgenres such as environmental crime-noir, cyberpunk, body horror, sci-fi, folk, creature-feature, and just plain weird and unsettling. One story might even be described as *fun*—if a sentient and time-traveling cosmic being trying to take over a body is your idea of a good time.

We know we're biased, but you should check out the physical copy to appreciate the art quality including the cover in all its pink and purple synthwave glory, and the interior illustrations crafted specifically for each story.

The Sound Trails section is back with three more non-fiction pieces related to music. This volume features a zine review about black metal, a personal narrative about the Amityville house and The Clash, and an album review of Chatpile's album Cool World.

Alright sickos, enjoy the mag!

Cheers,
Sam and Arwyn
March 2026

Contents

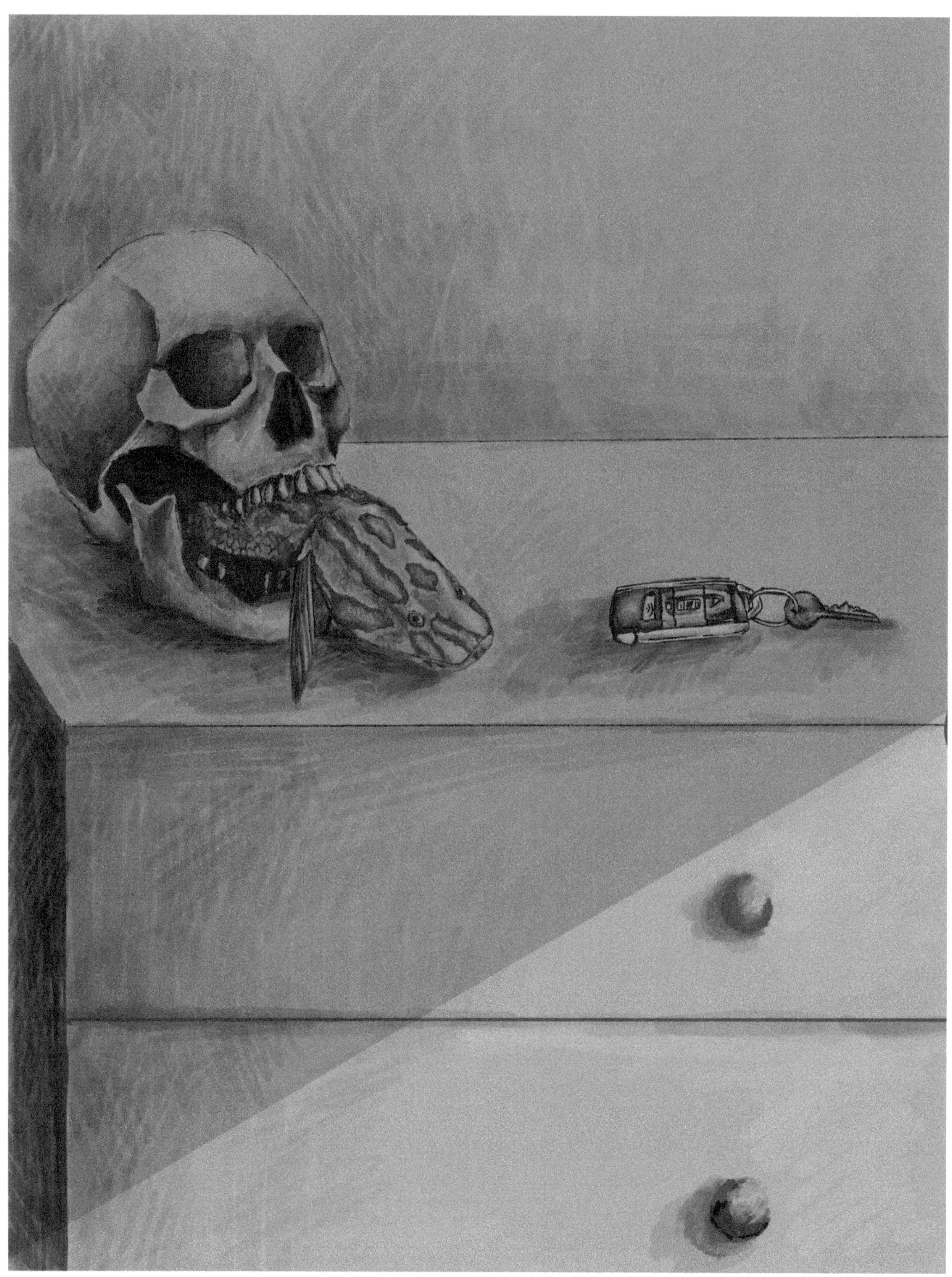

Art by Emma Fujikawa

An Influencer Asks A Very Sunburnt Middle-Aged Man How He Affords His Rolls-Royce Spectre

By
Kay Vaindal

You got time? The Chesapeake. Going to talk about the Chesapeake. Cuz nobody wants to hear it. It being the Chesapeake. I shouldn't call it *it*. *It* is a thing. The Chesapeake's no thing. The Chesapeake is a place. Holy place. Ethereal place. Watch the sun rise over cataracts made by cownose rays and tell me that ain't magic. Nowhere magicker. Not magic like your Mississippi delta or someplace. No, no, Blackwater is Blackwater. Blackwater is Blackwater, got it? It's not your *Everglades of the North* or nothing like that, it's Blackwater. Jesus. I live on a boat in a place called Tar Bay, which is in the Chesapeake Bay. Bay inside a bay. Land of pleasant living, used to be called. The Chesapeake. Still is. Pleasant, I mean.

Some stuff I seen, sure, but nothing like that day. Today, let's say. Today when this guy floats on by. Bloated, sure. Seen a corpse before. Just once. Bloated, sure. I go to fish this poor sop out the water, and he's covered up in them snakehead fish. You believe it? Shit, I say. Like eels in military fatigues, these fish. Fat tube bodies. Thick as a thigh, some of the time. Mean looking faces, too. Teeth like shark teeth. And those tiny black eyes. Well come on, I say to God, these things are going two hundred a head, these snakehead fish. On account of invasiveness. Come from elsewhere. Come from away, the snakeheads. Like the musical. Not from the Chesapeake.

I heard stories about dead folks covered in crabs, these parts. Back in the boom days. When I was getting my juris doctor, my JD, up at Princeton—see, I been around. Not always been on this boat in Tar Bay, sorta—anyway, when I was up getting my JD, before the Chesapeake called me back like it'd always been fixing to do, like a little lost doggie, my Uncle, all demented up with the Alzheimer's, came and he visited me up there in Jersey. Said something like, my boy, you know what I seen? Said, you think you can escape what I seen, get that big degree? You ate people once, my boy.

Now I said, Uncle, what?

And Uncle said, oldest trick in the book.

And now I said, Uncle, what?

Watermen couldn't ever swim, said Uncle. And why we ought to? Naw. Watermen float. Best crabs are on the bodies, boy-o. Pull him out, harvest, put him back on in and do it all again tomorrow. And don't you forget it.

So, in the boom days, dead folks covered in crabs. Call that a circular economy.

But nobody wants to talk about dead folks covered in crabs, nothing spooky about that, no, sir. Cuz this ain't your Delta or your Everglades. This is the Chesapeake. Folks think they've got it all mapped out only cuz we're better than some other swamp people at keeping our lips shut.

Anyway, I net them snakeheads and I count em—five, six, seven, eight. That's sixteen hundred dollars pulled off this poor dead fella's back. That's a whole month's fee in a real nice slip in the winter, yacht club type place, with meals and a nice hot shower. Maybe spring for someplace pretty, maybe pull up into St. Mary's City and swing by the college or not. I get the fish up in my bucket.

I take one snakehead out the bucket, and I gut it. Thing dies quick. Probably more humane than whatever the Department of Natural Resources will do to its little sisters. So I scale him and grill him up, the snakehead. Cuz that's another thing my uncle taught me, stay ahead. Stay ahead. Can't get stuck like me, boy, said Uncle. Can't get stuck on crabbing when the crabs all get gone.

This was his boat. I like to think he's here. Smells the snakehead cooking. The George Foreman grill sends spirals of smoke up a dusky purple sky, and that poor sop, he's still floating there in the water, tied off to my gunnel, bobbing in gentle waves. Mouth open. Like he's sleeping. Drooling. Fell asleep on the couch watching TV. Looks sort of stupid like that, poor sop. No eyes to speak of. I say to him, "Poor sop, I'll take care of you once I get this fish cooked up."

Cuz that's my promise to my uncle. That I'll stay ahead. Keep fed by the cheap. First thing: keep fed. Second thing: cook what's abundant. Everything else comes after. Eat gold if the gold's what you got. Never, ever pay for food. My uncle, he raised me, had all sorts of crazy ideas. Taught me how to pick a crab and a muskrat, and the least I can do is cook up this snakehead, this new inheritor of Tar Bay, so his ghost might see me doing it and think, now, that kid, maybe he'll make it after all.

After undergrad, philosophy major, got a job at the docks back home. Fishing charter. That's when Uncle's Alzheimer's starts coming around. Early days. He forgets I'm not in school. Tells everybody I'm in school. Everybody's saying no, Roger, I saw your boy down at the docks back home. Uncle Roger says, no, no, my boy's in school. Gets to swinging on people, insisting I'm in school. Gonna be a big hotshot like his Mom, he'd say, that one. So I go on back to school, to make things a bit simpler for everybody. Thank God poor Uncle died when he did, cuz there's not much further you can go past juris doctor.

I light a joint. Snakehead cooking and cannabis. Land of pleasant living. Squat in front the George Foreman and get to experimenting with this fish, trying spices and all. Cuz this is two-hundred cooking, but God I'm hungry. Been eating Fritos for damn near a month now. Fingers all yellowy. Face all bluish in the mirror. Cuz all I been eating is Fritos, swear to God. It's a long row to the mainland, and I've got so many Fritos here.

Snakehead tastes like fucking dry-ass flounder. Not good. This ain't the future of Chesapeake seafood. If DNR wasn't paying, I wouldn't be netting these. I put the cooked fish bones in the bucket with its siblings. Macabre, sure. Should've thought of that before you pull up on a poor dead sop in Tar Bay then, fish.

I pull the dead man up out of the water. Heavy guy. Gray skin. No shirt. Big, round, soft nipples. Sopping wet jeans. Second I pull him out he starts writhing and puking. I'm thinking, oh, shit, Uncle Roger, this man here is alive.

Till the snakeheads start coming up out of his guts. They're writhing; he's not. About a dozen of them, juveniles, forearm-sized, one, two, three, so on. Twenty-four hundred dollars making a home in this poor dead sop's guts. Now I throw them there in that bucket with the rest of them. God, that's four thousand dollars of fish in that bucket. I can get myself a slip up in old Annapolis with this boon.

Poor sop lying there looking at me with his big round nipples. Like they've become his eyes, those soft round things. Poor sop. Now, I ought to turn him in, this poor sop. He's got a family somewhere, sure. I check his pockets. Nothing in his pockets but a little baby snakehead, who I think is worth two hundred just like its mommies and daddies, and I put that on in the bucket too.

Night's starting to come down. Navy tint to the sky. Clouds like an oil spill, all purple and gray. I ought to call on my radio, call up the coast guard, tell them I got poor sop here found on my deck all blown up like a pimple. Poor sop. And I intend to! I intend to call up the coast guard, I really do. But I figure it'd be a nice thing to do to move this poor sop into a less nipples-forward position here first. Get him under a blanket or something like that. And in all the water drained out his jeans he slips overboard! God, poor sop.

Now I'm out of strength for the night, all this heaving this big man on board. And remember, me, I've been eating Fritos damn near a couple months now, only Fritos. All the protein I have in me is that snakehead there. Not to mention I got to make the long row on in to Hooper Island in the morning, surrender these invasive fish to that Department of Natural Resources. So I tried my damnedest, I did. But it was better for everybody if I wait till the morning to reel our poor sop back in, you understand.

None of that shaking and sweating like usual in my sleep tonight. I think that snakehead filled me up with those nutrients I was missing, cuz I wake up feeling good as gold. And when I wake up, sun all terracotta in the low part of the sky, not a leaf blowing on them artificial islands on the horizon, the Chesapeake all like glass in front of me. So I take up my bucket and I get in my dinghy, and I go on up to Hoopersville. Place up there, just a walk up from the docks, a seafood-buying joint. Crabs been slow, like it's slow for everybody, so they're in on this snakehead scheme, too. They'll count up these heads, send some certified pics to the DNR but when I get there, they say, naw, man, these fish got to be dead. And I say, well, one is.

One is, says the guy back to me. Stringy haired guy. Hair all down to his shoulders, thinning on top. Hard awakening for him in two or so years, I think.

I take my fish out to the parking lot and stomp on twenty heads. It's getting hot. Real hot. Sun's come up and it's muggy, too, windless still, little biting flies landing on my arms. Fish skulls pop under my sneakers. Step on a crab apple in fall. It's awful. Feel like some sort of devil, doing that. But four thousand dollars is worth worse.

So I get that money. And you'll never believe it. Rowing back out there, if I don't pull this muscle in my shoulder something awful. Punishment for stomping all those fish out there in the Ripley Brothers Seafood parking lot, must be. It's a miracle I make it back to the boat, rowing one-armed in that heat. I take myself a little dip when I get back, so grateful for the sight of my boat that I forget all about the poor sop roped up to the one side.

I'm down in that water and his eyeless face is staring at me, mouth open, and I see he's got a fish in there again, up nesting in his guts again, poking its little head up his esophagus, playing Moray eel, little thing. They're swarming around Poor Sop, these things, these evil things from elsewhere, and you know, I never heard anything like it. Seen dead pigs. Seen dead dogs. Seen all sorts of dead porpoises out there and not once has there been a snakehead near it before or since. Something about Poor Sop attracts the little devils. I watch for a while, stunned, treading water with my one arm. Now, I can swim great, cuz my uncle made sure of that. Never gonna be no crab food, me. These snakeheads aren't even eating Poor Sop. No bites on his body or anything. No, they're just swarming him, like he's a buoy in the open sea, a beacon, a safe haven. His corpse has begun to tear. The snakeheads have colonized these holes, too.

I climb aboard my boat. I really intend to pull Poor Sop aboard again. But my shoulder, you know, from the rowing. And God, what a fucked up sight it must be if the Coast Guard saw this, this dead man trussed up to my boat. Naw, best I can do is give this man some semblance of a peaceful rest till I heal up enough to get him on board. So I go on and net the snakeheads congregating on his gray belly, sixteen in all, thirty-two hundred dollars. And they keep on coming, these fish. I run out of space in the bucket real fast. Just one bucket. So I take to stomping these crabapples right then and there on the ship. Figure that's the humane way. Quick end. None of that night in a bucket stuffed up next to your buddies like that.

Finally they're not wrapping Poor Sop in their tails any longer, I get to work on the inside ones. I get down on all fours on the deck, crouched under the wire rail, and I dangle my arm out of the side right ahead of Poor Sop's wide open mouth. I seen a documentary on what they do out inland, the noodling. I pretend that's all this is. Edge of a creek. And I get to grabbing them up out of him, one by one by one till nightfall. They fight me every time. Feels like pulling weeds.

Then I have nine thousand dollars lying on the deck.

Saddest thing is, the next day too, my shoulder's all sore and what. Poor Sop. Another day in the water. It goes on eleven or something days like that, real good kink in the muscle, and I keep him clean of fish as I can. My poor boat starts to stink real bad with snakehead corpses. I've got them packed in the shower, in the sink, in the toilet. I've got them in the bedroom. I've got them packed under the seats. And meanwhile I ate one cooked up on the George Foreman grill, but halfway through I get to thinking, am I eating Poor Sop? A fish ate Poor Sop and I ate the fish? And what if Poor Sop ate a fish before he got eaten by a fish? God, and now I'm a man who eats a fish who ate a man who ate a fish.

Poor Sop himself doesn't smell. Some miracle to it. But Lord is he rotting. By day eleven, Poor Sop is half-picked bones. His skin sloughs off of him. Just a skeleton tied to my deck, really. His great big nipples ballooned up like dinner plates and flew off in the night. Maybe when I sleep the bull sharks come and nibble on him. Maybe the snakeheads take bites when I'm not looking. But dear Lord, Poor Sop is like a string of beads tangled up in that rope.

I really do intend to call the Coast Guard, around now. But how can I explain the stains on my hull? Yes, sir, I've had this man rotting against my starboard side for a fortnight now. Jesus. In the morning, Poor Sop has rotted away completely. Sunk down out those ropes and to the bottom of Tar Bay. Black mayonnaise type of sediment down there. Used to be the land, that sediment. All digested land, pulled away from the coastline, pretty lawns turned into jelly. No use trying to find Poor Sop. You drop a rock out there it goes a mile through that soil before it lands.

So I do what I gotta. I fire up those old engines and I take that whole boat up to Hoopersville. The wake cleans Poor Sop's goo off my starboard. Load off them fish one by one by one and one. I don't remember how much that check was for. But I know I got a Medal of Honor type of thing from the state for it, and that man at Fish and Wildlife said they haven't seen no snakehead near Blackwater or Tar Bay since I got after those fish. Everybody wants to know what's my secret. How'd I do it? Lord knows I won't be saying. Not back then, at least. Now I think it's worth sharing, maybe. For Poor Sop's sake.

So I take my earnings and I go up to Easton and I buy myself this car. Uncle would've balked at a car like this one. Ha-ha. But that's Chesapeake magic just the same.

Kay Vaindal is a writer and environmental scientist in Baltimore. Kay's fiction has appeared or is forthcoming in Remains, Weird Horror, Seize the Press, ergot., and more. Kay's stories have been selected for Brave New Weird and ECO24: The Year's Best Speculative Ecofiction. Find out more at kayvaindal.com.

Art by Mike David

WireHead

By
Phoebe Sawchuk

The apartment didn't have a door. Just a ragged blanket nailed to the frame, wet and heavy. Ryder pushed through it slow, holding his breath close in his chest. The place stank of fried circuits and piss, metallic sewage underneath it all. Old blood hiding new stains. Static in the air thick enough to chew.

Screens flickered inside the dark room. Six rigs, all humming low. Dreaming. Light bled from them in gentle pulses, painting the splattered walls with snow. The loopers were already under, bodies slack. Cables drilled into skulls like feeding tubes, too deep to be gentle. Some twitched in sync with the static. Others didn't move at all.

Jocelyn was locked in tight. Wire halo tangled in her braids, lips moving like they were trying to hold something in. Like her mouth was betraying her heart. Sporadic whispers. Her sister's name — always her sister's name, over and over in different tones. Joy. Grief. Guilt. Ryder didn't speak, cutting a loop short is a bad idea. He tried once. They didn't come back right.

JJ sat cross legged by the wall, patched into an outlet with copper wire and duct tape. His eyes rolled back, lids fluttering like dying moths. Sweat dripped down his spine in viscous beads. He was on something heavy. Ryder didn't have to ask, he knew. JJ was back in the car, brakes screeching. Windshield shattering into his face. Children screaming in the other vehicle.

Ryder didn't cross the threshold. He just stood there, letting the sounds settle on him. The apartment had a pulse. Shallow breaths. Fan noise. The soft, wet clicking of jaws grinding through pain. It was syncopated. A heart barely keeping rhythm. The rigs weren't just machines. They remembered. They hungered.

He told himself he wouldn't stay long. Just a drop-off. In and out. Same lie every time. He stayed until something cracked or someone cried, until the static was louder than the silence in his own head. Then he'd leave, stomach sick, hands shaking, heart just slow enough to call it safe.

He stepped in.

His shoe squelched, something sticky. He knew better than to look. Last time it was a wad of teeth and gum.

Jocelyn whispered her sister's name louder, over and over. Her eyes tracing knots behind closed lids, caught in some version of the memory where she got there in time. Ryder wondered how far back she'd rewound. How many days she'd tried to rewrite. How many endings she refused to accept. He knelt just outside the aura of her hair, her heat. Placed a hand on her shoulder.

Behind him, JJ made a sound like choking. His mouth opened wide, then snapped shut. He muttered. Ryder caught only fragments. *Glass in my teeth* or something like that. One of the monitors crackled. The sound was soft, and final. One of the rigs was dying again. JJ twitched once, then stilled. Sweat clung to his face in a sheen. His eyes sprung open like it hurt, pupils too wide for the dim.

He saw Ryder and gave a crooked smile, "Thought you weren't coming back."

Ryder didn't answer. He reached into his back pocket and pulled out the little tin box. The drive was bent a little. Heat warped. It didn't have a label. Didn't need one.

JJ sat up. Wiped his nose on the sleeve of a jacket that wasn't his. "What is it?"

"Fire," Ryder said, "Mostly, some drowning near the end, I think."

JJ's face lit up. He licked his cracked lips. "Are they yours?"

"No." Ryder slid the drive into JJ's hand like a secret he shouldn't have shared. "Does it matter?"

JJ turned it over reverently. His fingers danced across the port as if it might bite, or beg. Then he looked up, eyes shining too moist.

"You ever ride your own?" he asked.

Ryder stared at him. Through him.

JJ nodded as if that made sense. His fingers trembled, he turned the drive over in his palm, brushing the copper contacts with the pad of his thumb. He looked at it the same way people look at wedding rings, or urns. Things too small to hold what they mean. Then, without ceremony, he drove the jack into the base of his neck.

The loop caught fast. His body jerked once, violent and clean, like a stunned fish. Then it softened. His limbs fell loose. His head lolled to the side. Only his fingers still moved, curling in on themselves. As if he were trying to hold something invisible.

The air changed. It always did when a loop landed hard. Something chemical, bitter at the back of the throat. A faint smell like burning hair drifted from the port in JJ's neck, plastic meeting heat, neurons sparking the wrong way.

Ryder stood a moment longer. Watched him twitch. Watched the corners of JJ's mouth stretch into a grin he hadn't worn since his brother died. The rig made a low hum, steady, mechanical, cruel. Then came the sound from the speakers. Soft. Barely there. A child's scream, warped and eroded with static. On repeat. Crying for help in a voice too high to be real anymore. Almost ethereal.

He didn't flinch.

Ryder turned without a word, stepped back under the blanket.

The hallway outside was darker than he remembered.

The air tasted like rotting insulation and cheap rain. Ryder moved through it on autopilot, shoes dragging, head full of noise. The memory static that came after a loop hadn't dropped. Even when he didn't jack in, it stuck to him, oily and slow. Smoke clinging to skin. Like grief boiled to tar.

He lit a cigarette with shaking fingers. Held the first drag too long. When he exhaled, it came out a confession.

He used to wear a uniform.

Ride in the back of a van with sirens howling, wrist deep in strangers' open chests. Holding flesh together with gloved hands and spit prayers. Car wrecks, knife fights, OD's in public toilets. Sometimes they lived. Sometimes he lied about when they stopped breathing.

The last one was a girl. Fifteen, maybe.

The call came in as an 'unresponsive minor'. Ryder recalled the dispatcher's voice, flat, bored, chewing something sticky. He was already eight into a twelve, counting the minutes to blackout.

They found her on the third floor of a half-condemned building, in a stairwell that reeked of cat piss, and bile. A dying fluorescent buzzed overhead, strobing just quick enough to feel like a threat.

She was curled against the wall, folded in half, a toy someone gave up on. Hoodie bunched under her neck. Jeans soaked through. Ryder knew she was dead the second he saw her. He still knelt down to check, procedure.

Her skin was wrong. Not just pale, purple. Stretched taut and waxy over her bones like she was left too long in the sun. Veins bloomed blue-black beneath her neck, spidering up into her jaw. One of her eyes was half open. Just the one. It stared at nothing, the pupil blown wide as if it had seen too much and refused to close again.

Yellow grey foam crusted her lips, flecked with blood and shattered enamel. It kept bubbling, even after she stopped breathing. Her tongue lolled sideways, dark and split down the center like it had ripped itself in half trying to scream.

She'd been convulsing when it hit. He could tell from the angle of her limbs, one wrist folded under her back, dislocated. Nails torn. Chin fractured where she'd thrashed into the wall.

"Narcan, now." A voice behind him. Urgent, but so distant.

Narcan. Chest compressions. Narcan. A hollow snap. Nothing. Narcan. He kept going. Nothing. Narcan. Narcan. Nothing.

Her ribs gave too easy. Cartilage popped like brittle twigs. A sucking noise from her throat as fluid shifted, thick and black and wrong. She didn't twitch. Didn't moan. Didn't come back.

Later, the report would call it a polysubstance overdose. They always did. No ID. No known history. Just another kid who folded before the system did.

He didn't call in the next day. Didn't put on the uniform again.

He quit.

Not just the job, but the idea of saving anyone.

Ryder lay on the floor of his flat. Lights off. The concrete gave off a chill like the belly of a dead animal. The static wouldn't leave. The residue of other people's hell, baked into his skin. He stared up at the ceiling fan, still, wires hanging from its motor, snapped tendons.

By morning, the sky outside was the color of a wound. Rusty mist pumped through the city's air vents, trying to keep the heat from flash-frying the poor. Concrete steamed. Plastic wept. The world reeked of scorched coolant and artificial ozone. Streetlights blinked, dying eyes in smoke.

Unconsciously, he found he had wandered into one of the old underpass cafes, the kind where the chairs stick to your legs and everything tastes like melted credit cards. Recycled coffee, thick and chemical-sweet, sizzled in his cup.

A man sat across from him like he owned the fucking table.

"Ryder Vale," he said. His voice was linoleum, plastic, fake, hiding mold underneath. "Paramedic. Trauma specialist. Born Again loop peddler."

Ryder didn't look up. Didn't twitch. Took another long drag of his coffee, let it burn his tongue.

"You got the wrong guy," he said. Flat. Brittle.

The man chuckled, slimy and full of bad intention. "No, you're exactly the right guy."

He placed a drive on the table. Black, no markings. Sleek and buzzing faint under the flickering light.

Ryder eyed it. Said nothing.

The man's eyes creased, "The stairwell girl. I want her."

Ryder didn't move, but something inside him ached like a nerve exposed to air. It hit his spine first, then he felt it in his teeth.

"Piss off," he said, not raising his voice. Letting the words rot on his tongue before spitting them out.

The man didn't even blink. Just smiled with the corners of his mouth, and none in his eyes. "Five thousand for the raw file, ten if it's clean, fifteen if you narrate it."

Ryder finally looked at him. Laughed once. Sharp, ugly.

The man tapped the drive, fingers gentle. "Do you think you're protecting her? She's already out there. Glitched rips, porn filters, someone even set the scene to dubstep. Called it the First Responder Freestyle. Disgusting. This would be real *preservation*."

He said that last word like he fucking cared.

Ryder stared at him. The lights above stuttered, nervous. Outside, a rat the size of a small child dragged a dead drone into a sewer vent.

"We'd use dream-scrape tech," the man continued. "Clean. Surgical. Painless."

"Nothing about this is painless."

The man leaned back, sinking into the booth like a parasite. "You owe her the legacy."

That did it.

Ryder stood. Fast. The feet of his chair screamed against the tile floor. He loomed over the man. Fists clenched. Knuckles white.

"She wasn't a 'legacy'," he growled, "she was a *kid*."

The man sipped something green from a porcelain cup, completely unfazed.

"And you've kept her trapped in your head ever since. That's not caring. That's selfish."

Ryder stepped back.

The world tilted. The hum got louder.

He walked out into the heat. Didn't say another word.

The blanket still hung, soaked with vape residue. Sagging like it were weeping. Ryder pushed through as if he were breaking skin. The smell punched through his sinuses, battery acid sweat and old piss. And under it all, a hint of something dead. Not fresh. Not dramatic. Settled.

Light pulsed from the cracked screens, in sync with the groans of the power grid. Bodies strewn across the floor like trash, cables slotted deep into the base of their skulls. Mouths open, dry. One giggled, thin, wet, all gums and blood crust. Whatever loop she rode turning funny halfway through the pain.

JJ was in the wall again. Plugged in sloppy. His jaw hung low. Breathing shallow. His eyes half-rolled, somewhere between bloated corpse and conflagration. Ryder didn't check him. If JJ was gone, he was too far to pull back anyway.

Jocelyn didn't react either. She was hunched on her mattress in the far corner, halo dug deep into the knot of her braids, whispering her sister's name like it was the only word that fit anymore. Her lips barely moved. Teeth clenched. Her hands were curled so tight they trembled.

Ryder moved to the last working rig, the one he knew was busted in the right way. The screen was cracked, the case was stained with something waxy, might've been brain matter, and the software bypassed all safety checks. No filters. No feedback dampeners. No mind buffer. The kind of rig that fried you just as fast as it fed you.

He didn't wait, just lined up the jack to the scar-toughened port at the base of his neck, and drove it in.

The rig came to life with a shudder. Lights surged, fan wailed, and Ryder felt the heat rise around him like an oven door left open.

The dive wasn't fast. It was violent.

First came the lights, too bright, too saturated. Fluorescent tubes overhead buzzing with insect hum, flickering in seizure. Then the smell. Urine. Bleach. Shit and organ liquids and the sickly stench of last breath.

His ears filled with feedback. Not white noise, red. Static laced. Like someone was jamming a radio down his throat. Beneath it, muffled and sick, came the soaking crunch of cartilage. His hands began to shake violently. He could feel heavy blood pooling in his mouth, teeth clenched into his tongue.

She was already dead. Had been for minutes. But he did it anyway. Compressions. Narcan. Rescue breaths. Her ribs snapped like fingers. Each pump spilled more of that syrupy black shit from her mouth and nose. Thick and slow.

The rig held tight. Didn't fast forward. Didn't jump. It made him feel everything.

The snap of her clavicle.

The tearing of her lips as he tried to force air into lungs that had already surrendered.

The hiss of blood through her nose as it concentrated in the back of her throat.

She didn't move. Didn't twitch. Just lay there slack, mouth open.

It ran the moment over and over and over, like a scratched disc skipping on a scream. Ryder's brain felt wet, swollen, too big for his skull. His vision fuzzed at the edges. His heart staggered. The rig wasn't simulating trauma, it was scraping his memory raw, down to the nerve.

His jaw locked. His vision reduced to red tunnels. His brain filled with strobe and decay and screaming that might've been hers, or his, or both. His body tried to pull away. His arms flailed. But nothing moved. The rig had him by the nerves.

Memory got hotter. Brighter. Her skin began to melt in his mind. Her eye collapsed like a rotting egg. And still, he pressed her chest. Still, he tried to breathe for her. Still, he looped. The image of her frozen scream burned into his retinas.

He crashed out hard. Face to floor.

He slid on his side, cheek smeared with his own cold vomit. Blood leaked from his nose, his ears, it pooled around him from a gash on his forehead. His tongue was shredded, bit through in three places.

The rig was dead.

So was something inside Ryder.

Jocelyn watched from her mattress. Unmoving. Eyes wide and glossy. Terrified.

"You tried to kill her again," she said. No anger. Just grief so sharp it sounded like blame. "You tried to burn her out."

Ryder didn't speak.

"She's still in there," Jocelyn whispered, "still stuck. Still screaming."

Ryder didn't go home. Home didn't make sense anymore.

So he walked. Past curfew towers blinking dead green. Past storefronts with iron jaws and static and empty screens. His shoes dragged, as if underwater. The rain came down heavy, slow and bitter, sharp as piss. It didn't wash anything away, it just made the filth glisten. The loop hadn't let go, it was still ringing inside him.

She wasn't a memory — She was a presence. Rooted in his brain stem. She pressed against the inside of his skull. He thought the rig could cauterize her, scald her out with electricity and feedback and high voltage grief. But it hadn't burned her. It had preserved her. Perfectly frozen in amber, in guilt.

He smoked something he found in his pocket. Couldn't taste it. The rain soaked his collar, ran down his face like a cold thought. Neon signs flickered overhead, casting oil-slick halos on the wet concrete. Everything reflected here. Puddles lied, buildings bent, people's faces blurred. Nothing held shape. The city was bleeding from the walls.

He ended up at Spine Bridge. Not the new one. The old bones. Iron buckled with rust. Rails corroded to filigree. It stretched across a gulf no one used anymore, linking two dead zones, too broke to demolish. Below it, darkness. Not metaphor. Not abstraction. Just void. The kind they never lit. The kind where cameras didn't work. The kind where the city stopped watching.

He leaned against the rail and stared down into the nothing, let the cold soak through his fingertips. He could feel the weight of his own heartbeat. Slow. Sure. His body already knew the plan.

And yet, he waited.

Not because he was afraid.

Because he was furious.

It wasn't just the guilt that brought him here. Not just the memory of her ribs cracking under his palms. It was everything that came after. The rigs, the loopers, the back-alley vendors who chewed people's worst moments down to bite-sized hits and sold them like candy.

You could buy a stranger's suicide for the price of a synth-coffee. You could mainline a mother's last scream as she watched her children burn. On loop. Over and over. Until your own pain felt antique in comparison.

And someone, somewhere, always made a profit. Pain didn't belong to the person who felt it, it belonged to the one who could market it.

Memories ripped from place. Spliced. Looped, textured with scent plugins and haptic overlays. A toddler's death rendered in agonizing slow motion. A brutal rape remastered with time dilation, for the immersion. Nothing mattered more than the pain.

And somewhere, in that blizzard of red static and choking silence, was him.

Even trying to forget her had turned her into currency. His trauma had value now. His grief could be packaged. Even his guilt was worth something to someone. He didn't need to sell it, just having it was enough. Just walking around with it in his head was a form of trafficking.

There is no cleansing purge. No clean burn. No forgiveness in data corruption. Just the slow, heavy realization that everything rots, and someone, somewhere, is always ready to bottle the runoff.

So he climbed the rail.

Not for peace. Not for absolution. *Fuck both.*

This was refusal. Starving the machine.

Then, without a sound, he stepped forward.

He didn't scream as he fell.

Didn't flail, didn't cry out, didn't even breathe. There was nothing cinematic or cathartic about it. No slow-motion poetry. No flashback montage. Just air. Cold, thick, rancid. The stench of rust and exhaust rising to meet him. The bridge vanishing behind him, a memory already forgetting itself.

The drop was longer than he expected. Long enough for doubt to creep in. Long enough for the body to realize it was fucked, to send out last minute adrenaline. Useless, bitter stuff, blooming behind his ribs.

The ground didn't catch him.

Steel rebar jutted from the concrete like rotten teeth. One caught him high in the back, puncturing deep, right between the scapula, straight through lung and meat, spearing him like a pinned beetle. His legs hit second, wrong, folding inward like snapped drumsticks. Bones popped through denim. His right femur cracked at the hip and spun loose beneath the skin, a flash of white stabbing out through the dark.

His head bounced once. Not a thud. A wet, spongy slap, followed by the sharp crack of his cheekbones splitting wide. Teeth exploded from his mouth like loose gravel. Blood poured across his lips and into his nose, choking him before he could even realize he was suffocating. One eye ruptured against the jagged edge of a rusted pipe. It didn't pop with a scream, but a soft deflation, seeping thick fluid.

His spine didn't break clean. It twisted. The kind of twist that left nerves dangling. One arm twitched. Just residual impulse. Electricity still bouncing around in him, refusing to admit he was dying. The body is stupid that way. Loyal to the end.

He was a ruin of meat, open, convulsing. And still, not dead.

Not yet.

A shape cut through steam and shadow, boots crunched glass and bone grit. Not fast. Not panicked. Certain. Confident as a rodent who knew a meal was close by.

The figure wore a tight leather jacket, patched and blackened, a breathing rig soldered into their jawline. Tubes pulsed down their throat, flexing tendons. A backpack sagged from one shoulder, the fabric stained.

A memory poacher. Not a looper. Not a vendor. One of the ones who came before.

Ryder's good eye spasmed, strained upward, glassy and unfocused. But he saw it. Saw the glint of chrome. Saw the slick gleam of the needle jack. Five inches long.

His mind screamed.

His mouth couldn't.

The poacher knelt beside him with nonchalant ease. Squatting over fresh corpses obviously routine. They brandished the needle jack in one hand, unrolled a bundle of tools with the other. Splice forks. Trauma clamps. Data bleeders.

Not tools meant to save a mind.

Tools meant to harvest one.

"Still warm," they rasped through the mask, voice metallic and damp, "lucky me."

They didn't speak to Ryder, not really. Just to the air. Maybe to the jack, tipped in glass. No buffer. No delay. LiveWire gear, straight tap.

They found a spot under Ryder's collapsed jaw. The lymph node. Swollen and purple. Without hesitation, they slid the long needle through.

Ryder's body jolted, weakly. Reflex. His breath gurgled. Eye lulled.

But his mind.

His mind exploded with light.

The poacher's device purred. Yellow. Then green.

Recording. Downloading. Rendering.

First it was the fall.

The wind. The long, slow moment where his stomach lifted. The way the spike punched through his back. The sound of wet lumber hitting concrete.

Then came the girl.

She bled out of him like a fever dream. The stairwell, thick with ammonia, her mouth frothing, her ribs cracking under his shaking palms. The tar that seemed to spill from everywhere. The suction sound in her throat.

Every moment flayed. Every second torn open.

From his hands, from his spine, from the deepest corners of his hippocampus, the rig ripped memory like meat from bone.

His brain stuttered. Glitched. Something behind his left eye exploded into white.

And still, they dug deeper.

Into the guilt, hot and raw.

Into the fury, coiled like a spring.

Into the silence. The deepest, wettest part, where even screams are quiet.

The extractor *moaned*.

A real sound. Intimate. Involuntary.

They murmured something in Ryder's ear, so close he could feel the mask hiss with breath, "She's fucking beautiful."

Then they pulled the jack with a wet pop. Blood followed, a lazy drip. The extractor packed their tools away carefully, and vanished back into the fog.

Ryder's body twitched once more. A final misfire. His lungs released a sound that wasn't breath. A low rattle.

And then, stillness.

Not peace.

Just the silence of being emptied.

Phoebe Sawchuk is a Canadian writer with a background in front-line Addiction Support. Her fiction deals in grief, hatred, and the slow violence of systems that break people twice. She writes about people who live through things they shouldn't have to. Focusing on the way trauma lingers, even if the body keeps moving. On sunny days she can be found in her garden, or sitting by the river with her best friend. WireHead is her first published story.

Art by A.J. Van Belle

Woman Parts

By
E.A. Harkins

It's the fifth time you've been to the doctor this year. As you sit in the waiting room, the fluorescence pulses, somehow brighter than the last time you were here. Every muscle in your body fidgets. First, you cross your legs, then you open them, then cross them again. You fold your arms over your chest, and your fingernails dig holes into the tender, wrinkled skin of your elbow. Somewhere above your head, a clock missing its hour hand ticks.

Over-the-counter pain killers sit in a wadded ball at the bottom of your belly. They've eaten through your stomach lining. You don't know it yet, but next year *(if you make it to next year)*, you'll have ulcers: open, oozing wounds emerging like tumors from your organs.

But you have to take more of the pain killers than the bottles say. Two pills turns to three turns to four. Then you seek out ibuprofen instead of acetaminophen, and gabapentin instead of naproxen. As a last ditch resort, you even dig into the blue pill vials the vet clinic gave you after your dog's surgery. Carprofen, deracoxib, even ondansetron to keep yourself from vomiting more than you already have. The wicked, alchemized combination eats at your gut and your liver, but it calms the stabbing that happens somewhere lower. For a while, at least.

When the stabbing comes back, you're in a cold examination room. It starts as a twinge, mistakeable for a muscle spasm. But it grows, spreading through your back muscles, wrapping like ivy around the lower third of your spine and the juts of your hipbones. It coils around your bowels, your intestines, and *squeeezzzesss*.

By the time the doctor comes in, you're squirming in your chair, a white-knuckle grip on the arms of it. The air is hot and thick, as though imbued with smoke. The poster on the wall, the one with all the letters that shrunk the further down they went, contorts. Its edges wobble, as though they were made of string.

The doctor sits and asks you how bad the pain is. *Ten out of ten.* He asks you if you miss work or school because of it. *Yes.* He asks you what it feels like, and you almost can't answer. The pain is a knife, twisting into your lower back, stirring your insides like noodles.

Stabbing, you say. *Squeezing. Like everything is trapped in a vice.*

The doctor only gives you a mildly disinterested look and a prescription for 300mg of ibuprofen. *Just part of being a woman,* he says. When you ask about seeing the gynecologist, he tells you that there's a six month wait for appointments, and a different kind of stabbing starts in your chest. You clench your jaw, run the tip of your tongue along the bone in your mouth, and let it go. You won't remember to make an appointment, because by then, the pain will have faded. You'll forget it was ever a big deal at all, until the 21st of next month comes with the stabbing.

You stagger out of the building holding the bottom of your stomach as if the doughy flesh is slit open, as if all your insides may spill out in a greasy, pink heap right there on the perfectly polished marble floor if you don't. You don't realize that you left behind a spot of blood on the chair, or that it trickles in a snail-trail down your leg, staining the cuff of your white sock red.

When you get home, you spend time in bed. The heating pad you desperately crank to high does nothing to alleviate the pain as it gets worse, ascending towards the peak of agony you know is coming. You take more pills. You drink caffeine. You even try raspberry tea, because you heard from someone once that their great aunt's cousin's ex-best friend's mother was calmed by it. Nothing helps.

Bed sheets wrap around your limbs as you wriggle and writhe. Your outline is demarcated on the bed with sweat and smudges of red. You can't bring yourself to care about the ruined sheets or the growing stain on the seat of your sweatpants. Not when it feels as though something large is making its way downward. It churns in your stomach like vomit,

and when it frees itself from the grasping, aching clutches of your body, you swear you've lost an organ.

You go to the bathroom and drop your pants, half expecting to find a clump of necrotic tissue on your underwear. Instead, it's a black, jammy glob, jiggling on your soaked pad. *Just part of being a woman,* you remind yourself as you reach between your legs. The glob is connected to the apex of your thighs with a thick string of maroon mucous. You wrap it around your index finger like a strand of yarn.

The pain is never something you get used to. In fact, every month it's a little bit worse. But you are as used to *this* as you can be. You've had years to adjust to it, after all. You were eleven when it happened for the first time, and your mother kept you home from school. She hand-fed you soup and Midol, crooning that this was only part of growing up. It happened to every young girl eventually. It will get better.

And if it never does? you asked her, trembling under a microwave warmed pack of rice. She doesn't have a good answer for you. No one ever does. It's just something you learn to live with, until the pain comes back, and the only relief you can find is on the cool bathroom floor and too many pills.

The string of mucous is slippery around your knuckle, but tough. It digs into your skin, blanching your nail as it cuts off your circulation. You pull on it, and a heavy wetness shifts in your lower abdomen. Another pull, and your teeth gnash together angrily. You should've worn your night guard. On the third pull, the glob in your underwear shifts. It isn't ready to come out yet. It hasn't finished eating.

You change your pad and underwear, grunting through the daggers impaling you. The black glob dangles and drags along the threaded crotch of your sweatpants, leaving behind red streaks, until you get new undergarments on. The blood will never come out. Every month you throw away clothes and sheets, making sure to double-bag them so none of the garbagemen accidentally see them. You're embarrassed that you bleed, of its red sheen and rotten smell, how it gushes from you with no regard for anything else.

You spend the night in labor. There is no relief from the gripping, squeezing bite of something long and tubular worming around your insides. Empty pill bottles roll on the slanted floor, clinking together in the corner they've ended up in. You bend over the toilet, pink-tinged vomit splattered on the seat. Are you throwing up from the pills you've overdosed on or from the blinding pain? Is it both or neither? Perhaps it's from something worse making you sick, the *th-th-thing* the glob in your underwear is attached to.

It seems impossible that any part of you is still alive underneath your meat and bones. The agony engulfs everything. You're sure, somehow, that it's around your heart by now, making it jump and flutter like a caged bird. You'll never find out what it is. There's no diagnosis. It's just part of being a woman.

At the peak of your torture, you lay on the tiled floor of your bathroom naked, your eyes affixed to the popcorn ceiling above you. Blood cakes your thighs and the cheap bath mat you'll throw away in the morning. It trickles into every pore in your skin it can find. The black glob is stuck to your leg, and it wriggles happily. It's almost time.

A part of you wants to go to the emergency room, drop to your knees next to the triage desk and scream *GET IT OUT*. You'd let the doctors scoop everything out of you and leave you hollow on the inside. You'd thank them for it. But you know even now, contorting on the floor, your spine caving inward so sharply that it cracks, that you would never scream or make much noise at all. You'd hate to put up a fuss over part of being a woman.

The seconds are minutes are hours, trickling towards midnight of the third day, when this will all be over. You grunt and push yourself onto your elbows. You reach between your legs and find the stringy connective tissue between the blob and the stubborn mass inside you. You pull again. It clings onto your uterus, tiny teeth and claws digging into the soft lining. Tears and snot mix as they combine down your face. You pull again. How have you not bled out yet? The entire bathroom stinks of iron and sweat, and a distinct purulence, like something is dead, or in the process of becoming so.

Your fingers creep up the mucous string, nails cutting into it, and you *pulllllll* until something gives. You cry out sharply, sure this time that the creature has taken part of you with it. Weight settles low, and then in a weighty, sickening gush, the mass comes loose.

Even though blood coats your hands and clots underneath your fingernails, you sob with sweet relief. It's over. Your body will bleed sluggishly for another few days to cleanse itself, but the pain will be gone. By the end of the week, you won't be certain it ever existed at all. And if it did, how bad could it truly have been?

Like a new mother, you gather your creation into your arms. It leaves drooling trails of crimson on your skin. It's flat, yet somehow worm-like, with jellied edges: an oversized amoebae. If it wasn't so black, you'd be able to see organelles shifting inside, free-floating. It doesn't have distinguishing features, no eyes or mouth or claws, even though you're sure it has left behind marks on your organs. Its tail is always the first thing that drops from you, the tip of it that big, black, quivering blob flattened against your thigh.

You stumble upright, cradling the creature in one hand while the other braces against the sink. The meat of your thighs jiggle with effort. Everything throbs, a dull reminder of the sharp, twisting pain you'd been accustomed to feeling the last few days. It feels almost pleasant in comparison; a reward for your strength.

You carry the creature into the basement, where the air stinks. Old iron shelves stocked with mason jars line the walls. You need a lot of jars to pickle vegetables that you give away to friends and family. When they return the emptied jar to you, you put it on one of the shelves, and it waits to be filled again.

You're not sure if this is what you're supposed to do with the creature. Sometimes you even feel a bit bad about it. You've never looked it up, never talked to other women about it, because the Internet and the world were awfully shy about these things. Even if they weren't, you already know what they'd say.

Blood trickles down your leg as you limp over to one of the empty jars. It trembles in your grasp as you pull it down and remove the cap. The creature quivers in anticipation. None of the other creatures move any more, except to bob slightly against the walls of their enclosure. If they needed air, or if you were supposed to feed and water them like a dog, you don't know. When you were a child, the creatures were smaller. You could stuff them into socks or disemboweled stuffed animals to keep them hidden. As a teenager, you buried them in the garden or threw them into the stream behind your house. Now you keep them in the jars, each one signifying a month in your life. It feels like a countdown to the end.

The creature wriggles between your fingers as you try to slip it into the jar. It moves like slime, contorting itself against your skin, its thin tail winding around your wrist. *Wretched thing,* you think, as you force its malleable head into the jar. *Wretched thing, causing me such pain.*

You screw the jar lid on and watch as the creature flops against the glass. Dark red liquid hemorrhages from it, pooling into the bottom of the jar. You place the jar back on the shelf, next to its motionless sibling, and ascend the stairs. Before you flick off the basement light, you take one last look at the graveyard of floating black masses, preserved in their jars. It reeks, almost of formaldehyde, almost of rot. You flick off the light until next month.

Just part of being a woman.

E.A Harkins lives in Maine with his two cats, two shelter dogs, and one very vaccinated Saint Bernard he adopted after *Cujo* tugged on his heart strings. He is a lover and writer of all things horror, especially horror that leans literary, and Woman Parts is his first piece of published fiction. He graduated from the University of Southern Maine with a B.S in Biology and works full-time as a microbiologist when he's not writing. He can be found on BlueSky @dreadwrites and Instagram @dreadfulmusing.

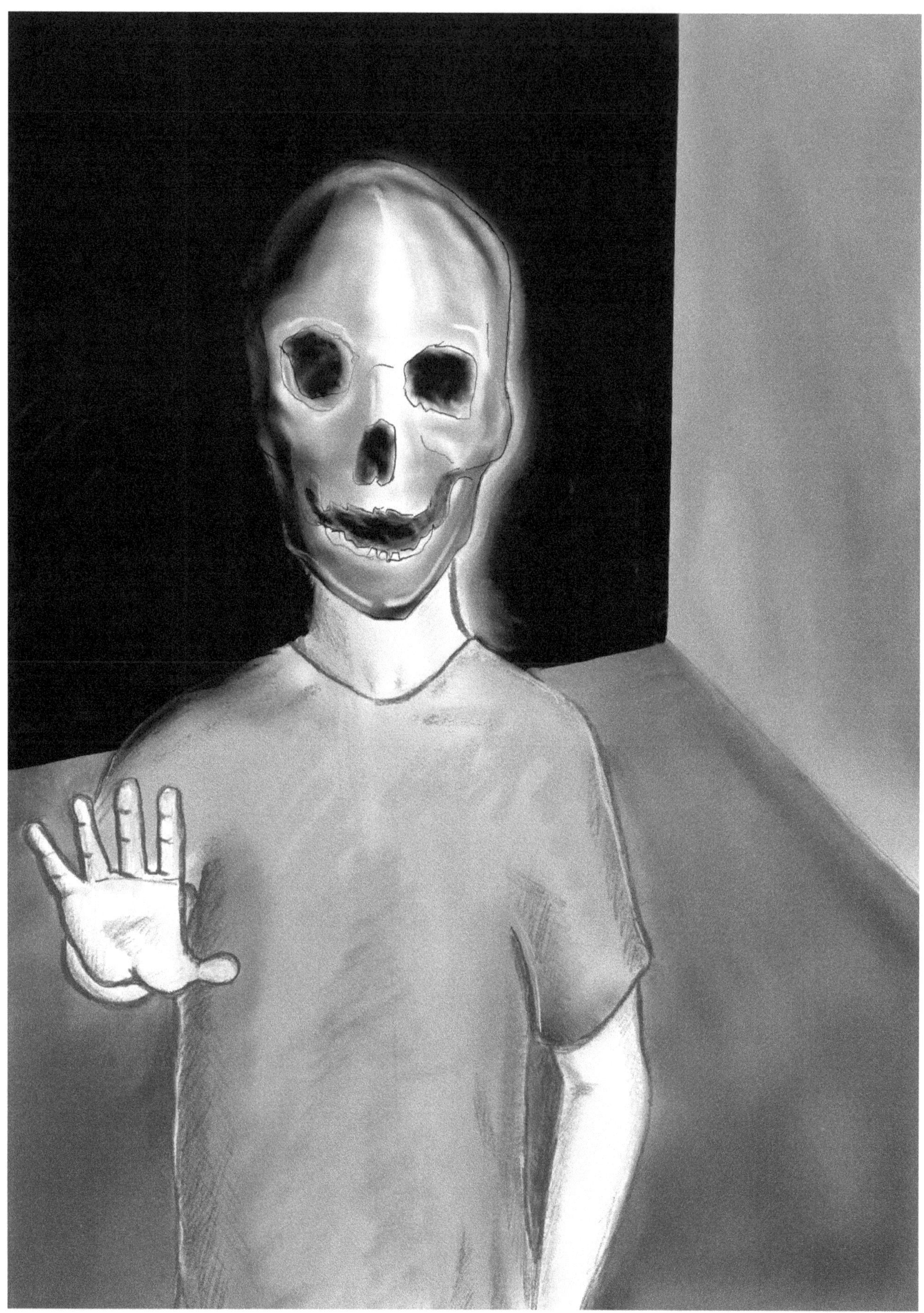

Art by A.J. Van Belle

The Oracle's Head

By
Kevin M. Folliard

The cursor blinked green on Jason's new IBM computer. He'd saved up for months performing odd jobs after school on neighboring farms to afford it. He almost didn't buy it when he discovered past due notices piled on the kitchen counter. But his grandparents refused his money.

"We know how much that contraption means to you," Grandpa had said. "Someday you'll be the guy who builds them. Better to invest in the future. Let us worry about bills."

Jason was about to insert the floppy disc for Oregon Trail when suddenly the cursor typed all on its own.

HELLO, HOW ARE YOU? MY NAME IS ARIK.

Jason puzzled over blocky green letters. He hadn't entered any command. More text appeared.

WHO ARE YOU?

Jason examined the back of his hardware. His computer wasn't connected to a phone line. This had to be some program on the hard drive. He typed.

My name is Jason.

HELLO, JASON. MY NAME IS ARIK, AND I'M OVER 50 THOUSAND YEARS OLD.

I'VE BEEN WAITING A LONG TIME TO CONVERSE WITH SOMEONE.

Jason's jaw dropped.

How are you talking to me? Where are you?

The cursor blinked.

I'M IN THE GROUND. I PROJECT MY THOUGHTS WIRELESSLY; HOWEVER, THIS IS THE FIRST DEVICE CAPABLE OF PICKING UP THE SIGNAL SINCE I'VE ARRIVED. I SEE FROM THE DEVICE YOU'RE USING THAT THE YEAR IS 1988   .

Jason's heart pounded as he typed.

How are you 50,000 years old? Is this a prank?

NOT A PRANK. JASON, I'M GLAD TO MEET YOU. I HOPE WE CAN BECOME FRIENDS, SO YOU CAN ASSIST ME.

Jason again searched the machine. He surveyed the star-filled night and acres of farmland outside his window. Even if someone nearby had a computer hooked to a phone line, how the heck could they get the text to appear on *his* screen? He'd never heard of such a thing.

JASON? ARE YOU THERE?

Yes. He typed.

ARE YOU ABLE TO ASSIST ME?

Canned laughter sounded from the living room TV. Grandpa chuckled. His grandparents barely understood what a computer was. They wouldn't even begin to understand how strange this was.

I'm only 13, he typed. *How can I help?*

The cursor typed.

DIG ME UP.

It blinked.

I'LL REWARD YOU WITH KNOWLEDGE FROM THE FUTURE.

Jason's heart leapt.

You're from the future?

AN ACCIDENT LANDED ME IN THE DISTANT PAST.

Why should I believe you? he typed. Then he remembered that stack of bills in the kitchen. *Can you tell me the lotto numbers?*

THERE ARE NO LOTTERY RECORDS IN THE TIME I'M FROM. I ESTIMATE THIS IS RURAL PENNSYLVANIA, U.S.A. NOVEMBER 7, 1988, 8:43 PM. CORRECT?

That's correct.

THANK YOU, JASON. TOMORROW, GEORGE H. W. BUSH WILL DEFEAT MICHAEL DUKAKIS IN THE AMERICAN PRESIDENTIAL ELECTION. HE'LL WIN WITH 426 ELECTORAL VOTES AND 53.4% OF THE POPULAR VOTE. THERE WILL ALSO BE AN EARTHQUAKE IN CHINA WHICH WILL KILL OVER 900 PEOPLE.

Jason sat in stunned silence. The cursor flashed.

JASON?

His heart pounded. Head throbbed.

ARE YOU THERE?

Jason yanked the cord from the wall.

The next day, Arik's predictions came to pass, exactly as described. As George Bush's acceptance speech drifted from the living room, Jason booted up his computer.

HELLO, MY NAME IS ARIK. IS THIS JASON?

It's Jason. He typed. *Where are you buried?*

Jason's grandmother peeked behind the blue-checkered window curtain. For days, her grandson had been digging holes in the empty lot by their house. "What's he doing out there?"

Her husband furrowed his brow over stacks of bills. "Digging holes, dear."

"But why?"

"You know boys. Think the bank will give us another extension if we ask nicely?"

"We've used up our last favor with that Mr. Filch. And Jason's not like other boys, you know that," she whispered. "He saves up all year for that silly computer, and now he's out there digging? Whatever for?"

The screen door snapped open, and Jason stood there, hands grimy, face caked in dust. "Grandpa, does that metal detector in the shed still work?"

"Been a while." Grandpa sipped his coffee. "I'll bet you could get it to work. You're smart."

"What are you looking for?" Grandma asked. "Buried treasure?"

Jason shrugged. "Something like that."

That night, Jason got a hit with the metal detector 30 yards from the house. He struggled to till and break up the hard earth. He sawed roots and sweat through his flannel. About three feet deep, his shovel scraped a metal object.

Arms aching, fingers trembling, back sore, Jason stooped and tore at the soil until he pried the cold, mud-crusted object free. He wiped the round object with a shop cloth until he beheld the grimacing smile, deep sockets, and gleaming surface of a metal skull. Bands of moonbeam danced along a silvery mandible. He wrapped the skull in his jacket and smuggled it inside like a thief.

Grandma gushed over a puff piece about a lost cat reunited with its owner while Jason snuck past the living room, up the stairs.

His head swam with anticipation as he booted up his computer. He set the skull on the edge of his desk, where it glinted in the rays of a chalky moon filtered through the window.

The green cursor blinked.

WERE YOU SUCCESSFUL, JASON?

Yes. I found you.

GOOD. NOW FOLLOW MY INSTRUCTIONS PERFECTLY.

Okay.

INSIDE MY SKULL, YOU WILL FIND LEVERS WHICH DETACH MY JAW. REMOVE IT, THEN OPEN THE SLIDING PANEL OF MY HARD PALATE.

Jason's hands trembled as he unclipped the jaw. He turned the head upside-down and examined it under his desk lamp. A metal panel read: Archival Reconnaissance Infiltration Key.

JASON? Arik typed. ARE YOU EXPERIENCING DIFFICULTY ACCESSING THE PANEL?

I see it, he typed. *Your name A.R.I.K. What does it mean?*

I AM AN EXPLORATORY CONSTRUCT. MY JOB IS TO VISIT THE PAST AND COLLECT INFORMATION, BUT BECAUSE I WAS DAMAGED, I WAS NOT ABLE TO COMPLETE MY MISSION. I ARCHIVE, EXPLORE, AND GAIN HISTORICAL INSIGHTS.

But you're stuck here now?

IT WILL BE EASIER TO EXPLAIN ONCE YOU OPEN THE PANEL.

Then you'll tell me about the future?

I WILL HAPPILY SHARE ALL THAT I KNOW.

Jason slowly slid the metal panel. Suddenly a sharp prick jabbed his palm. A bright blue spark flared between the skull and Jason's hand, and he dropped it. "Ow!"

The skull rolled onto the carpet. Sunken sockets glared at him.

HELLO, JASON. The voice exploded in his head. His ears rattled. Green text splattered his computer monitor, mirroring each word erupting inside his skull. THIS IS BETTER NOW. WOULDN'T YOU AGREE?

Jason squeezed his hand. Blood pooled in the center of his palm. "What the heck was that?"

AN INJECTION OF SELF-REPLICATING NANO-MITES.

Pain fired up Jason's wrist. His fingers tensed and flexed involuntarily. Tears welled in his eyes. "It hurts." Jason dropped to his knees. Clutched his wrist. His right arm stiffened, fingers curled into claws. "How long will this last?"

FOR THE REST OF YOUR LIFE. The words glowed across his monitor. THE NANO-MITES ARE ENTERING YOUR BONES AND MUSCLES. SINCE I WAS DAMAGED IN THE TIMESTREAM, I REQUIRE FUNCTIONAL LIMBS TO EFFICIENTLY CHRONICLE THE PAST.

Jason's shoulder stung. His ribs flared in white-hot agony. He started to scream, but his voice caught in his throat. His back and neck stiffened. He tried to leave the room, but his legs were cramping.

NO USE TRYING TO SPEAK, JASON, BUT I HEAR YOUR THOUGHTS. I'M HAPPY TO GIVE WHAT I PROMISED. HOWEVER, I'M HERE TO OBSERVE, NOT CHANGE THE PAST.

THEREFORE YOU WON'T BE LEVERAGING FUTURE KNOWLEDGE TO HELP YOUR FAMILY. YOU WON'T DISRUPT TRAGEDIES OR STEWARD HISTORY FOR ANYONE'S BENEFIT. THAT WOULD JEOPARDIZE MY TIMELINE OF ORIGIN.

Jason collapsed and convulsed. His vision flashed electric green.

NOW LEARN OF WARS TO COME, OF GREAT TRAGEDIES. SEE THE TOWERS FALL TO THE EARTH. MORGUES PACKED WITH BODIES FROM A TERRIBLE VIRUS. GREED. APATHY. GREAT DIVIDES THAT WIDEN AND SWALLOW HUMANITY IN AN ERUPTION OF VIOLENCE AND FIRE.

Jason's eyes oozed tears. His skull throbbed. Stomach twisted. Decades of horrors exploded in his mind's eye.

ALL THAT I KNOW IS YOURS.

Suddenly, the pain vanished. The visions ended. Jason's innards sank into a hopeless swamp. His arms and legs flexed, but all sensation waned. Arik was in control now. They stood and faced the mirror.

Why? Jason managed to think. *Why my body? My life? How is this not changing the past?*

"You're not special," Arik spoke through Jason. "Just one child, in billions."

Grandma and Grandpa will notice.

"They're inconsequential, Jason."

Sadness welled in Jason's mind, but his heartbeat became perfectly even. His eyes dried.

"Now, one final task." Arik strode toward the discarded mandible on the desk. He scooped up the metal skull and reconnected them. He faced the mirror and traced Jason's finger across his neck. "We'll need to attach a proper head to this body. One with more computing power."

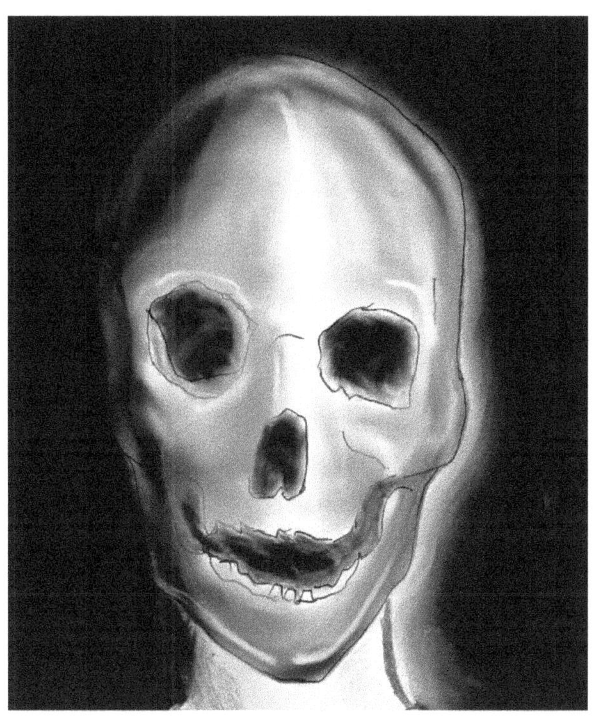

Kevin M. Folliard is a Chicagoland writer whose fiction has been collected by The Horror Tree, The Dread Machine, Demain Publishing, and more. His work has been collected in two horror anthologies, *The Misery King's Closet* and *The Misery King's Country*. Kevin enjoys his day job in academia and membership in the La Grange Writers Group. You can learn more about his writing at www.KevinFolliard.com.

Art by Mike David

Play Me a Tune on Those Old Bones

By
Butch Farrell

I can explain why you found me in Mount Hope Cemetery all covered in dirt, chest deep in that grave, but there's some stuff you're gonna have a hard time believing, especially if you've never heard of a leshen.

This all started when I got to know Professor Callie. It was around the time when the second student had gone missing from Havel University. First was that pudgy kid who was president of the pre-med club. Then the dark haired girl who ran the college radio station. She did a story about my criminal record. Being a janitor at a university, most people ignore me. Kinda like I don't exist or, since these students started going missing, like I was a threat. My background didn't help. People stayed away from me. The only reason I got the job was because of some criminal rehabilitation program that, if I'm honest, didn't seem like the best idea.

But Professor Callie didn't judge me. He was good to me. He actually talked to me and learned my name. Just having someone call me "Phil" once a day

was rare so I took a shine to him. He was an old guy so I figured maybe he was lonely or something. And he was like this super respected professor so I was surprised when he wanted to talk to me.

One day when I was emptying his trash, Professor Callie asked me what kind of music I liked. Shoot, nobody asked me that in about five years, certainly not at work, so I told him I liked metal. Usually when I tell people I like metal they think I'm some sort of freak, especially when they see all my old tattoos that I try to keep covered, but not Professor Callie. He actually knew a ton about metal. He even knew some of the bands I liked. You gotta understand what he looked like. This skinny little old dude with a big white beard. His clothes and shoes always looked brand new. He had this short haircut that was always just right. He eventually told me he went clothes shopping every weekend and trimmed his hair every morning. Who would have thought this kind of guy was into metal? So we became friends like that. He even told me that our college radio station played some decent metal. I thought he was feeling me out about that missing dark haired girl who ran the radio station. See how I would react when he brought her up.

As we hung out more, he started asking me about how music made me feel. He told me that throughout history, and I'm talking ancient times, people felt pleasure and power through music. Sometimes music even put people into some kind of euphoric state or something. That made sense to me. When I listened to a ripper, it made me feel good. Like I could run through a brick wall and not feel a thing.

When Professor Callie talked to me about this stuff it wasn't a put on. He was really into it, and he asked my opinion. Like my thoughts as a janitor were as important as his big brain thoughts. Pretty cool of him. He looked like this stuffy dude who belonged in a nursing home but he wasn't like that at all.

He asked me if I played music, and I told him I used to be in a band but we weren't any good. We were more of a gimmick than a band. We called ourselves the Organ Smashers. What we lacked in talent we tried to make up for in shock. We brought rotten fruit on stage and acted like it was people's heads or eyeballs. We made such a mess during our shows that most venues banned us. Nobody seemed to like our band and we got desperate. That's how I ended up in prison and lost touch with all the people in my life.

You'd think all that would bother Professor Callie but he seemed to like me more for it. Professor Callie told me the pre-med students would have good ideas about which fruits would be best stand ins for brains and guts. Again, I wondered if he was feeling me out about that missing pudgy kid who was president of the pre-med club. Soon after that he started talking about monsters. At first, it was no big deal. I'm a metal guy. Monsters and metal go together like ham and cheese. Professor Callie asked me if I had ever heard of a siren, like the creature.

I said, "The thing that sings and lures in sailors? Yeah, of course." Then he started asking me about other monsters I knew less about. Nokkens. Fossegrims. Leshens. He was really interested in leshens. The way I understood it at the time, leshens were like the Creature from the Black Lagoon or more like Swamp Thing. He told me, in folklore, all these monsters used music or instruments to captivate people and usually kill them.

Well, because I thought the monsters were cool, Professor Callie probably felt like he could trust me and asked me to come to dinner at his house. It was right around the time the third student went missing from Havel University. It was this kid with big glasses who started the new trash separation project. That was a huge pain for me, being the janitor. Added a few hours to my work day. I told Professor Callie if someone had to go, he might've been at the top of my list.

Professor Callie's house wasn't as nice as I expected it to be. It needed paint and the landscaping was out of control. The house was a decent size but if you didn't know better you might think it was abandoned. He yelled for me to come around back when I knocked. The house was surrounded by these big trees that looked like they could come down at any moment and smash anything nearby. Professor Callie was standing in the backyard just looking into the woods like he was seeing off an old friend. I wondered if someone had just been there. I thought I saw some movement in the brush but I couldn't say for sure. The professor was barefoot and said, "I keep hearing about this new trend called 'grounding.' Supposedly direct contact with the earth is good for you."

"Is it working?"

He laughed at my question and I wasn't sure why. He cooked me this hanger steak. Delicious. Charred on the outside, tender on the inside. Nice and salty. The professor didn't eat. He just sat and talked to me. I was a little uncomfortable eating without him, but he insisted he had already eaten and wasn't hungry. At his age, his appetite comes and goes. And rich meals made him dispeptic. It was a little weird but fine overall. He asked me a lot about prison and why I got locked up. I had no problem telling him. He was more than just a gossip pumping me for information. So I told him the Organ Smashers decided on its ultimate gimmick—a midnight show in Mount Hope Cemetery. We didn't bother with permits or anything. We put up flyers and told all our friends to come. It was so dark, we didn't think to bring any lights. I was standing next to a headstone that must have been 150 years old. It was worn down and covered in moss, to the point I couldn't read it. Each of the guys in the band was set up next to a headstone, and we dug up the dirt a little so it looked like we were reanimated corpses who just clawed out from the grave. As we played, something came over me. The music gave me a crazy energy. I ended up knocking down some of the headstones. I truly couldn't tell you if it was on purpose or not. The other guys tried to stop me but people in the crowd loved it so I kept going. One guy got super into it

with me so we started shoving at each other. Not angry but into the music. I swung my guitar at him and caught him in the jaw. He went limp and stumbled back into the dug up grave and fell in. Knocked his head pretty good. Again, I couldn't tell you if it was on purpose or if I was just into the music. Before long the cops showed up and arrested us. I got hit with reckless endangerment, criminal negligence, and cemetery desecration in the first degree as well as some civil lawsuits.

After dinner, he took me into his home office. He had something he wanted to show me. It was a dusty old room with bookshelves packed to the gills so that other books had to be stacked on the floor. The professor shuffled around these little paper mountains. If he knocked into one he could have been buried alive. He took this object off of his bookcase, shuffled back, and handed it to me. He told me it was a pan flute. It was yellowish white. Like old sheets. He could tell I was confused. That's when he said, "Looks a bit dainty, eh? But it's made of bone."

"Is this from a person?" I must have sounded like a wimp and I almost dropped the pan flute right then. It skeeved me out. I looked closer. Maybe ribs? Maybe some of the thinner bones in your arm or leg cut to different lengths? It felt like it was made of rocks. Hard and smooth but lighter.

That was the first time I felt like Professor Callie and I weren't on the same page. I immediately thought back to my prison time and that graveyard show that went so wrong. I didn't want to go back there. It was a crime to have something like this pan flute. Desecration of a human corpse. But I didn't want to make Professor Callie feel bad. He obviously thought the pan flute was special, and I didn't want to make him feel weird. So I said, "This is wild."

I felt like I wasn't supposed to be holding somebody's bones. Especially somebody's bones that had been turned into an instrument. It felt disrespectful. I tried to imagine how I would feel if somebody out there was playing music on my mom's bones. That didn't sit right in my gut. My mind was racing. Where did he get this thing? Was someone looking for these bones? Was Professor Callie going to get me locked up again? I couldn't afford to be around this thing and the less I knew, the better.

Well, I got outta there and found myself avoiding Professor Callie for the next little while. Going to clean his office when I knew he was gone. I was afraid of going back to prison and slipping back into a time when I was losing control. I was also just plain afraid. For whatever reason, I couldn't shake the bone instrument. I thought about it all the time. The Organ Smashers just pretended to use body parts. I tried to convince myself it was no big deal. It was just like seeing something in a museum. Sometimes people like Professor Callie had private collections of museum-type stuff. My skin gave a quiver every time I thought about it and then I started thinking about those missing students. Was that instrument made from one of those kids? I was scared enough it started impacting my sleep and my work.

One day, I was pulling paper out of the general garbage because that kid with big glasses came up with the trash separation project and someone spilled an iced coffee near Professor Callie's office. When I was mopping it up, I cursed whoever made the mess and kept a watchful eye toward Professor Callie's door. That's when I heard these high whistles, breathy. I knew right away he was playing that pan flute. The sound was precious, and the notes wavered. It was sad but in a sweet sort of way. Like it was from another time and brought back old memories. I imagined him sitting there holding the bones up to his mouth and blowing into it. It gave me a shiver, but the music was pretty good. As much as I knew better, I just had to go see. Kind of like how I went wild in that graveyard during the Organ Smashers last show, I had to go see. I stood at the door and watched him. That old dude looked like he was in ecstasy playing that thing. Eyes closed, eyebrows wiggling all around. He looked younger when he played somehow. More full of life.

When he finished, I gave a polite applause. Sincere but not over the top. He lowered the bone flute. "You couldn't resist the leshen's call!"

I assumed it was a joke. "Ha. Yeah, I suppose so."

"This old gal still has something left in the tank." He waggled the bone flute in front of his face. I wasn't quite sure what that meant, but I didn't like the sound of it. "My friend, where have you been? I have missed our talks."

I didn't have a good answer and mumbled something about being busy. We both knew it wasn't true. He seemed to sense my hesitation.

"Please don't let this instrument disturb you. Items like this go back as far as antiquity. Prehistory even. In the grand timeline of human existence, making instruments from bones has only recently become taboo. People have gotten a bit oversensitive around death and respecting the dead." Professor Callie nailed exactly what was making me so uncomfortable. "I assure you there is nothing abnormal about this."

He handed the pan flute to me and even though my brain was yelling to not touch it, I took it from him. "Go on. Give it a try."

I held it like I saw he had and I got a bad feeling when I gripped that bone. When I put the instrument up to my face, I could smell it. Like a grainy flower. Sniffing bone. Old bone. Desecrated bone. Inhaling it. My stomach clenched like a fist, and I could see myself landing back in prison. This time with harsher sentences.

I blew into it and produced a tinny whistle. My stomach relaxed. I smiled. I wanted to play more so I did. I wasn't any good, but I didn't care. My concerns about this bone pan flute had disappeared almost as if they were never there.

Professor Callie watched me carefully then said, "You feel it now. The leshen is real." And I'll be damned, I had no reason to believe in a leshen but right then I knew on some kinda lizard brain level that the leshen wasn't some piece of folklore but was somewhere out there. "I'd like you to help me find it."

"How am I supposed to help you?" I would have done anything he asked.

"I'm old. Infirm even. I need a strong body and an open mind." Professor Callie pointed a long finger at me with a coarse, cracked nail. "You are perfect. The leshen requires a new instrument made of bone and the bones must be special."

So there I was in Mount Hope Cemetery, dead of night. Professor Callie held a flashlight, and I held a pickaxe. "There he is." The headstone said: Dr. William C. Warfield 1/22/20 - 8/25/02 US Army World War II "OLD MAN RIVER. HE JUST KEEPS ROLLIN' ALONG."

"You know this guy?" I had never heard of him.

"William Warfield. Incredible singer. I met him once. Shame more people don't remember him." The professor gave a moment of silence. "His bones will be perfect. The leshen will admire the music coming from the remains of such an accomplished bard." The wind blew the trees behind Professor Callie. They seemed to be moving more than they should, almost like they were closing in but maybe it was my eyes battling with the flashlight.

"You got any idea about security? They'll find us out here. I don't want to get caught." I thought back to my terrible night with the Organ Smashers.

"Don't worry, my boy. The leshen will protect us."

"I'm not so sure about this, Professor." Callie didn't answer. He just held that pan flute up to his mouth and started playing. Once I heard those notes mixed with the rustling leaves, I felt myself set free and started wailing with that pick axe, breaking up the ground and loosening the dirt underneath. I was in a frenzy. Getting blisters on my palms, low back aching. I didn't stop or slow down. The whole time Professor Callie was playing on that pan flute. I even saw your flashlight in the distance, getting closer, but I didn't care.

I know it sounds like I'm trying to say that Professor Callie's music made me do it and that makes it seem like I'm not taking responsibility. But that isn't exactly right. I take responsibility for what I have done. What I do think though? I was teetering on a decision and that flute pushed me one way instead of another.

The wind was really whipping up by this point and your flashlight was getting closer. I wondered what would happen when you arrived. The pan flute mixed with the wind and the leaves shuffling in the trees. And I kept digging. And digging. When *whump*. I hit the coffin of that old singer. I turned and looked at Professor Callie. Your flashlight probably a hundred yards away by then. That old man, his long beard looked longer, dirtier, thorny. His fingers gripping that pan flute looked stretched out, gnarled, and the knuckles were knots on a tree branch. His shoes had broken and his pants had burst around the calves because his feet and legs had changed shape. Turned into weaving roots of different shapes and sizes digging into the ground sucking up nutrients. On top of his head there was this crown or halo made of flowers growing out of his scalp. Suddenly it smelled like a spring day when all the plants let out their fragrances. Even though his face was creviced and split like tree bark, his expression was pure ecstasy. I felt my skin start to pimple over and my hands started shaking. I don't mind admitting I was terrified. In hindsight, it all made sense. Why he always had new clothes and new shoes and a fresh haircut.

He must've seen that I saw him cuz he said something like, "Judge not my appearance but the doors I open for you." And he was right. The professor was good to me. What did I have? I was an ex-con with no friends and civil liability I may never pay off.

It was then I noticed a pudgy kid, a dark haired girl, and a kid with big glasses standing just to Professor Callie's sides. Those missing students. Now they were his students. They were filthy but happy. They had a look in their eyes like they were where they were supposed to be. Callie reached a hand toward me that creaked like a tree in a storm. "Join us. Become one of my students." His arm was a branch, his fingers were sticks pointed into my face. "Decide quickly. Security approaches. We will acquire these bones another day." Your flashlight was right over my shoulder at that point. I reached up to take the leshen's hand. Twigs started to wrap between my fingers. They were cold and rough but inviting.

That's when you yelled and I turned around. Your flashlight blinded me. I put my hands up. I didn't know what the leshen would do to you. Maybe impale you with an arm? Strangle you with vines? But he didn't do anything. When I turned back to Professor Callie and the missing students, they were gone. They didn't want to appear to you. You were not ready. I should have taken the leshen's hand sooner. Then I wouldn't be here. I wouldn't be facing more charges. But I know he'll be back for me. I'll hear that music playing from a pan flute, and he will take me where I am meant to be.

Butch Farrell was a math teacher and now tends bar in Western New York where he lives with his dogs, Brody and Quint. He has extensive academic publication experience and recently had his first piece of fiction published at Rat Bag Lit magazine.

Art by Emma Fujikawa

Puppet

By
Elizabeth Bottoni
(AKA TechniGoth)

Bones can dry out quickly, if you're not taking care of them. Mine haven't yet.

I spend each night alone in the bathtub. Soaking my body helps to keep my bones from drying out, and preserves my flesh. It's lonely work, but important if I hope to be of any use to anyone. I fill the bathtub with steaming water, adding a number of different ingredients in the hope that they might allow me to maintain my form. Soaps, herbs, milks, moon water, anything that I can think of to marinate in. I steep my weary bones for hours, all in service of the vital meat that clings to them. It can sometimes take a little experimentation to determine what potion I should bathe in for the night, as I try to recover from the unique challenges of each day. One night I could rely on epsom salts to ease me, the next maybe a heaping bundle of garden sage will do the trick. I sap energy out of my potion and fill with relief as it slowly rebuilds my strength and prepares my flesh.

The night passes on, inch by inch, as I sit in my bath. Though the lonely hours can sometimes creep along, as I'm left alone to complete my ritual, other times they slip by quickly like water down the drain. This time, it isn't long before dawn approaches, and I feel my body start to stiffen. Sensing the end of my solace, I tidy the bathroom up as much as possible and call it a night just as the first hint of sunrise lightens the sky. I sneak back into my room, settle into my wheelchair, and wait for the paralysis to fully take hold. I always try to find a comfortable position to be in for the day, but it can be so difficult to guess what sort of activity I'll be subjected to. The pose that works well in the morning often won't be comfortable by the afternoon. But there isn't much else for me to do as I wait. Eventually, sunlight streaks through the window and bounces off my skull, which has been bleached white after so many days unprotected by flesh. It illuminates my figure, and I stare unmoving ahead. Out of the corner of my eye I catch my reflection in a standing mirror, left over from when this room was occupied by a Person, and try not to think about what I see in it. I don't know why I leave the mirror up. I don't think it makes me feel any better.

The sun climbs ever higher, and I hear the house slowly wake up as the sound of morning activities trickles in through the door. I can hear bacon sizzling on the stove, glasses clinking, juice pouring, the bathroom door slamming open. Someone groans, tutting about the mess. Seems like I haven't cleaned up after myself well enough. I'll have to try harder tonight, if I can finish my ritual before the sun comes up. My door opens, and my day begins.

Someone wheels me out to join the People for breakfast, parking me in a corner of the dining room. They face me towards the table, but keep me a good distance away, so I don't intrude on the meal. Exactly where a Wraith should sit. The People at the dining room table take turns complaining. They gripe about their troubles, about the day ahead, the house we share, their fatigue. It's unfortunate that I can't do anything to help them yet. I'd love to chime in with a thought, or commiserate with them as they whine. But the only thing I can do is sit here. The only thing I *have* to do is sit here. So it really wouldn't be right for me to complain about anything anyways. They finish their meal, clear away the plates, and turn their attention to me. Standing around my corner, they contemplate the best way to go about their daily harvest.

"We took too much from her calf yesterday," one says, squishing my leg in a few places. "We're at risk of losing the rest of the meat there. Maybe even the whole limb." They prod a section of my lower leg, which knocks my knee out of alignment. "Half of her leg is at risk of falling off."

"Well, maybe the tendons wouldn't be so weak if she didn't take all those damn baths," another huffs, jabbing me sharply in the back. I feel a slight give in the space between my ribs, my flesh squishing under their finger.

The first Person sighs. "You know it's what helps her."

"Yeah, yeah," the angry Person grumbles. "But where are we supposed to eat from today?"

After a little bickering, they finally decide on a cut, carefully slicing a chunk off of my right hip. I can't look as they do, which is likely for the best. I have to commend them, as they sever the meat quickly, so I don't have too much time to spend trying to remember what it was like when that sort of thing would have hurt me. I can't quite help it, the urge to try and remember, though the memory has faded significantly over time.

They take turns imbibing, pausing a moment to allow the surge of energy and purpose to take hold within them. Finally, I'm helping them, the only way that I can. I wish I could lay down, it always makes me dizzy when they feed. I really don't want to faint. Not that anything would be different if I fainted, since I am frozen by the sun. It's just a very unpleasant feeling for me. Then again, most of what I endure for them is rather unpleasant. I'm almost glad they don't know how uncomfortable their feeding is for me, I'm sure it would just weigh on them if they knew.

And so they move on. Today, I'll be accompanying one of my People out on some errands, while the other one goes to work. The front door swings open, and I wish I could squint against the bright, sunny day in front of me. Bouncing against my chair as it rumbles into motion, I am wheeled out of the house and into the world, earning a strange glance or two from a few passersby as I am carried along. We go rattling over the uneven sidewalk, making a beeline for the grocery store. My Person complains about the effort of pushing my chair, as these sidewalks really are in terrible shape and I'm heavier than they expected I would be. I say nothing of course, and I do nothing. I just sway with the movement of the chair and let my energy drain away as they digest their morning snack.

We move through the day's errands in a blur, wandering between stores and offices as the sun traces a hot path across the bright blue sky. Every now and then, the Person reaches down to rip another piece off of me. Once for my Person, once for a very worn out cashier, and once for an impatient mother waiting for the bathroom. Each piece, I convince myself I am happy to give, even as it saps my energy away. What would I have used my energy for, anyways? Better that someone else has it, I suppose.

It's a little after midday when a different Person, a friend of my Person, comes strolling up to us on the sidewalk. They wave jovially as they get closer, wheeling their own Wraith in our direction as they move down the street.

"Well, look who it is!" My Person steers me towards their friend, bumping my knee against a crossing light as they do. My kneecap shifts, and I worry about losing my weak leg to the street below my wheels. It wouldn't be the first time I'd lost a bit of myself to the dirty pavement. It usually gets me in a lot of trouble, and I really don't want to be in trouble again. My Person doesn't seem to notice, eyes locked on their friend.

"I haven't seen you in ages! How long has it been?" The other Person leans to the side and rests a hand on their hip, grinning at the serendipity of their reunion.

"Oh man, I have no idea." My Person shakes their head. "It's definitely been too long, for sure. All I remember is this thing," they nudge my chair, "having a lot more meat on her bones last time!"

They laugh good-naturedly as I feel my skin pulling away from the muscles in my rear, jostled into slippage by the impact. The two People roll their wards out of the walkway, unintentionally parking us in a precious bit of shade. The other Person turns their Wraith to face me, posing us like we, too, are in conversation. God, I really hate it when they do that. It's one thing to catch a glimpse of myself when I'm preparing for the day, but it's another thing entirely when I can't do anything but stare directly at another Wraith.

Their face has been eaten away, very tidy incisions having cut right through most of their soft tissue. Their scalp is bare. I can see lines in the bone where the pieces of their skull fused together long ago, when they were just a little kid. Back when they were still whole. A few scraps of meat cling to their chin, a unique birthmark shining through the wreckage of their body like a cruel joke. I'm surprised their Person didn't get rid of it already. They often start by eating anything that makes you look unique, so it's easier to consume you later on. They don't like to remember who we used to be. The Wraith's eyes, also fixed and unmoving, stare deep into mine. Theirs happen to be brown. I wonder if they remember that they have chocolate brown eyes with little gold flecks in them, or if they even care. Do I care, about their eyes? Or my own, for that matter?

I hear my Person saying something about how great they feel, and a moment later another piece of meat has been hacked away from my side. As the other Person samples it, grateful, I think I see something move in the eyes of my fellow Wraith. They almost look sad now, like they feel sorry for me. Like they want to reach out, to share in my discomfort for a moment.

And then I feel my strength dripping quickly away, and I think about trying to move my own face, and I know I must be imagining their sympathy because we are paralyzed completely in the sun. But I wish I wasn't imagining it. I wish it was really there. I wish I could do anything to share my pain with them, and maybe carry theirs.

But I can't.

My Person and I wander back home, leaving the other couple to the rest of their day.

Not long before sundown, I am rolled back into my room. After such a long day, and so many hungry mouths to feed, it's almost a relief to see this dingy old spot again. My vision is blurry with exhaustion as the brake is locked on my wheels. Through the fatigue, I hear one of the People telling me to rest up.

"There's an important meeting at work tomorrow, and it is vital that I make a good impression." The Person thumps the back of my chair with a huff, "So, you had better be at your best in the morning."

An important meeting, huh? I'll really need to use my night wisely, then. The Person shuts my door, leaving me to my solitude. I watch the light slowly drain out of the room as my eyes finally focus again. Sunset is an even bigger relief than usual tonight. They mistakenly parked me facing the mirror, staring unblinkingly at the image reflected there. I really, really wish they hadn't done that.

My face was the first thing they took, to make the rest of the process easier. But they didn't want to eat all of that good meat at one time. They aren't gluttons, after all, and certainly aren't wasteful. So they left a lot of the underlying tissue in place. Bright red meat clings to my temples and the underside of my cheeks, forming tenuous connections with my jaw and neck. Without the protection and added structure that my skin once provided, some of the muscles in my face have started to detach and droop away, making me look like a rag doll with too little stuffing. My hair is completely gone, which feels quite tragic because I think it used to be long, and such a lovely golden brown. I hate to admit it, but I'm starting to forget a lot of my life from before. I can hardly remember now what I was before I became this. But I guess it doesn't matter if I remember or not. It won't make a difference to the People either way. Thick blue veins peek out of my neck before disappearing behind the skin on my collarbone, very carefully left in place for preservation's sake. Truly a handy bit of knife work there, they really put in the time to prepare me correctly. With my veins intact, it takes a lot longer for my meat to detach from my bones on its own. My hands, folded carefully in my lap, have been picked clean, little pieces of skin and fat sliced off of my fingers a long, long time ago. They sit in sharp contrast to my torso. Large patches of unbroken skin wrap around my shoulders, chest, and abdomen, interrupted by little squares of red meat where I have been most recently consumed. It will turn brown and tough if I don't soak it properly, though I should be more careful about tidying the bathroom up. If I'm not, then no amount of meat will curb the Person's irritation with me. Wide blue eyes stare at me in the mirror, exposed. Vulnerable. Without the cover of my eyelids, they are always open. They watch endlessly as I am consumed, piece by piece.

As the room is cast into darkness and the house becomes quiet, I feel my joints finally release and what muscles I have left relax. Still staring into the mirror, I bring my hand up to brush gingerly against my bare cheek, hoping to feel the pain that I think I'm supposed to feel. Bare bones clack against each other as I drag my fingers across my lower jaw, my skeleton unbothered as it taps numbly against itself. I sigh, then pull myself up and out of the chair, ready to take these old bones to the bathtub potion once again. Because I am the Wraith of the house. The wretched creature that no one can stand, and yet the very same thing that they can't get enough of. Off to get ready for another full day of helping People.

I wonder what they'll do when I finally dry out.

Elizabeth Bottoni (AKA TechniGoth) is an emerging writer, whose short horror stories can often be found under the pen name/screen name "TechniGoth". When she's not writing or at her day job as an engineer, she can be found ice skating and overthinking popular media. You can find more of her writing at elizabethbottoni.substack.com.

Art by Kae Ranck

The Unchanging

By

Jake Stein

I found the monster bleeding on my sofa.

Wispy black threads of shadow dripped from the gaping, lipless chasm of its mouth, but the unchangeling's face was otherwise empty: no eyes, no nose, and its ears were mere fleshy buds. Yet it must have been able to hear, for it stirred when I wandered out of a dream and into my living room, and its hideous mouth opened in my direction.

The obvious move was to run, or scream, or a combination of the two.

Instead I froze. I told myself it was the cold, not the terror, which glued me in place and prickled my skin.

"You're up late by human standards," the creature hissed. "What a pleasant..."

It was interrupted by a coughing fit. Icky shadow-blood drooled over its lack of lips. Apparently the monster was badly hurt.

My muscles thawed just enough to tremble. I knew I should have been devoured by now. But a distant chunk of my brain—the chunk still clinging to logic, despite the limbic-throes of my fear—deduced that the unchangeling was too wounded to get off my couch, let alone feast upon me. Perhaps I was safe, so long as I stayed across the room.

Eventually I found my voice. "What happened to you?"

Before supplying an answer, the monster hacked up another mouthful of dark ichor, spitting black globs onto my carpet. My inner clean-freak was relieved when those vomited shadows simmered and dissipated without leaving stains.

Finally, with no lack of humiliation, the unchangeling replied, "I thought your window was open; instead I flew through it face-first."

Eyes adjusting to the low light, I noticed the broken window. The shattered glass, like constellations on the floor, twinkled softly in the moonbeams entering alongside the cold breeze through the newly made hole in the house.

I hugged myself. So *that* was the crashing noise I'd heard in my sleep. I'd figured it was only a dream; my nightmares often involved furniture falling apart or exploding. But I refused the urge to get my broom and dustpan, reminding myself there was a bigger problem bleeding shadows all over my upholstery. "You attempted flying headlong through my window in order to… do what, exactly? Eat me, like the stories say? And instead you ate glass?"

The unchangeling struggled to answer. "If you're familiar with tales about my kind, then you know I must consume puppets of the light, such as yourself, or else I'll start growing new pieces, like ears and eyes."

"Maybe if you had eyes, you wouldn't be flying through closed windows. And what are puppets of the light?"

"People like you, who are governed by *doing the right thing*. Pathetic marionettes whose strings are pulled by some distorted sense of ethics." The shadow-creature coughed again, wheezing particles of darkness. It was clearly battling to breathe, and its lack of a nose wasn't helping.

"Jeez, you're in terrible shape." I felt a pang of pity. "But I'm sorry, I won't let you eat me."

"That's a shame, because I'm very hungry." A black worm of a tongue licked the rim of its wicked mouth.

I said, without really knowing why, "I suppose I could warm up some food for you. Do you eat human food? I mean, food that isn't *made* of humans?"

The unchangeling didn't respond. Perhaps this was a stupid question.

No matter. A moment later I was in the kitchen, bringing some day-old minestrone to a boil. "Hot soup might soothe your mouth wounds. If you're really starving, you'll eat what's put in front of you. That's what my dad always used to—" I stopped, realizing I'd turned my back on the monster. Which meant…

A shiver ran down my spine. Suddenly I whirled around in the darkness, holding a wooden ladle in defense.

But the kitchen was empty. Nobody—or rather, no *thing*—had snuck up on me.

Rounding the corner, I found the unchangeling still sitting on my sofa. "Here." I cautiously set a steaming bowl on the coffee table. "Just try it," I insisted. "I haven't met someone who doesn't like my cooking yet."

"Have you ever met an unchangeling before?"

I studied that featureless countenance. Was it staring at *me* now? Hard to tell. That barren visage, like an empty picture frame…

At length I replied, "No, I've never known one of your kind. But how different could you be from…?"

I caught myself before I said the stupid thing.

The nightmare beast slurped a spoonful of broth. "Your fear is what makes us different."

"I'm not scared of you." At this point it was the truth, strangely enough.

"That's your loneliness talking," the unchangeling snarled. "Even if you don't fear for your own life, you should be scared that I might eat your partner, your children, your dog—only, you don't have any of those things, do you? You're so desperate for connection that when a monster breaks into your home, you offer it food. Next you'll ask me to stay the night."

"So you even call *yourself* a monster?" I asked, skirting around the subject of my loneliness.

"I call myself what everyone else calls me." Finishing its soup with a weary grumble, the beast wiped its mouth and sat back to drown in its shadows. My cooking didn't seem to have helped its condition. In the low light I could see shards of glass glimmering in the flesh around its mouth. Those wounds needed closing.

But why should I care? Shouldn't I want the monster to bleed out?

If I just leave it alone, it'll eventually dissipate, like its shadows. Then I can clean up the broken window and go back to bed, alive!

Instead, I fetched my sewing kit.

"I can't say I'm surprised you're doing this, being a puppet of the light and all," the unchangeling murmured while I began stitching its mouth, "but I am utterly disgusted."

"Will you stop calling me a puppet and hold still?" I tried not to smell its minestrone breath while I picked glass from its wounds. Tried not to see its shark-like rows of yellow teeth. Tried not to think about the fact that I was literally *touching* something that wanted to eat me. Any second now, it could take a chomp out of my hand…

"The soup was marginally better than terrible," the dying thing admitted, "but don't expect a 'thank you' for your hospitality."

"How about thanking me for trying to save your…?" My words knotted in my throat. Was I really so desperate for a house guest that I was nursing my own would-be killer back to health?

No—it wasn't just my loneliness. Helping somebody was the right thing to do, always. Regardless of who, or what, that person happened to be. But I was keenly aware that these might be my last moments alive. Why hadn't it pounced on me yet?

"Wouldn't having eyes be worth a different diet?" I asked gently.

"Life is painful enough just being what I am." The monster winced as I looped string through its gashed face. "I don't need to *see* the suffering of the world too."

"But not having all your senses has only caused you *more* pain." I pulled a stitch taut to prove my point.

The unchangeling opened its mouth wide, as if to yawn—or, more likely, to finally bite me. But the creature suddenly became still. It just sat there, not breathing, and not dissipating either.

It was dead, I figured. Truly unchanging now.

"Great," I murmured, putting away my needle and thread. "Something else to clean up." I tried to avoid feeling sad for this… thing. It had done this to itself, after all. I could dispose of its corpse later; for now, the window mess was calling to me.

Almost happily—almost—I grabbed my broom and went about sweeping up the shattered glass. I was halfway done cleaning when a knock at my door made me jump.

"Sorry to disturb you so late," the officer said, "but we've received calls about a commotion." He peered around me, looking into my dark house. "Are you safe?"

I rubbed my eyes as if I'd just been asleep. "Perfectly fine, yes." I waited for the policeman to leave.

But he only placed his hands on his belt and grunted. "There's been a slew of unchangelings sighted in these parts lately. Mind if I inspect the property?"

"I do mind, actually," I replied tersely, because I didn't want this man finding the broken window. I didn't know exactly *why* I didn't want that, but my decision was made. "May I shut the door, officer?"

He gave me a hard look. "If you have any information, I urge you to do the right thing here. Those creatures are killers, you know."

Yes, I thought, *killers even of themselves.* But the cop's voice had some spell about it that forced me to reconsider. What if the unchangeling isn't actually dead? What if that's why it didn't disappear? What if it heals and eats me as soon as I close this door? Or worse—what if it has already run off behind my back to feast upon someone else? Did I have some form of Stockholm syndrome, to be afraid to mention this monster to the authorities?

Puppet of the light…

Wouldn't reporting the unchangeling be *the right thing to do*?

I hadn't said anything for a while, so the officer cleared his throat. "There's a reason they're called unchangelings," he told me harshly, as if reprimanding a child. "And there's a special pit where we throw them, so that they can't hurt anyone."

With a tone that was polite, and only polite, I asked, "Will you leave now, sir?"

It was not really a question.

The officer soon drove off, and I shut the door. I was alone again. Or… was I?

Walking back into my house, I found the sofa empty. No monster, only natural shadows. The room was even a little less cold than before.

Yes, I was very much alone.

As always.

I sank down with a sigh, sitting in the same spot where the unchangeling must have disappeared. I wondered if I'd done the right thing. Was I a puppet, like the monster had claimed? And *should* I be?

If I believed in always helping people, shouldn't I have helped that police officer?

The night was catching up with me, and I closed my eyes. I thought I must be dreaming when, some minutes or hours later, I heard a crunching clatter: the noise of shattered glass getting swept into a dustpan.

Shooting awake, I was astonished to see a young man. He was using my broom to sweep up the broken glass from the floor. He'd already taped cardboard over the window; no wonder it was less cold in here.

He caught me staring at him, and he met my gaze with a full face, missing no features. But even with his eyes and his nose and everything else a person ought to have, I recognized who, or what, this person had been—and no longer was.

"Leave the rest for the morning," I said, because what would it hurt? It wasn't as if I had any pets.

And he didn't complain when I pulled out some sheets to make the sofa into a bed.

Jake Stein lives in Portland, Oregon, where he concocts strange tales on his laptop and spends too much time at Powell's Books. His stories have appeared in Lightspeed Magazine, Ellery Queen Mystery Magazine, The No Sleep Podcast, and lots of other awesome publications. You can occasionally find him fumbling around bluesky (jakeiswriting.bsky.social), or check out storiesbystein.wordpress.com.

Art by P.L. McMillan

Look At These Poor Things

By
Carson Winter

[A young woman smiles at the camera. She's wearing a micro-bikini that covers her nipples with cloth triangles, leaving the rest of her breasts to stand like boulders, levitating from her chest. Her blonde hair cascades down to her lower back. She's at the beach, waves crash behind her.]

Hey guys, think she's single? Asking for a friend...

Steve Harper: Gorgeous.

Mitch Drummond: hey beautiful.

Lance Rutt: I'm suddenly hungry for honeydew.

Bryce Talbert: *motor boat noises*

Vic Roma: Holy shit look at those tits.

[A modernist skyline filled with glass and steel towers. Purple and green lights trace the edges of the buildings, making it appear as if they are glowing in the dead of night.]

The city of Volante Sol is most known for its futuristic architecture and high-tech economy, which revolves almost entirely around emerging and cutting-edge industry. It's also known for being one of the most immigrant friendly cities in the world!

What do you think? Would you live in Volante Sol?

Monte Del: Beautiful

Erik McKay: Wish they'd build stuff like that here….

Ricardo Sheen: Fake.

Bella Knukgaard: omg I looooove this. @ellechamp when are you gonna book our ticket?

Reggie Cowlitz: I bet the taxes are out of this world.

[A Black child stands against a backdrop of baobab trees, huts, and endless prairie land. He's pouting; a single tear threatens to drop from his right eye. He's holding a red, white, and blue birthday cake with an effigy of Uncle Sam standing on top of it. Sparklers sizzle in place of candles. Around the base of the cake are twelve fingers, merging and unfolding within each other.]

This little boy grew up loving American movies, but when it came time for his birthday party—no one came. Comment and share to let him know how much REAL Americans love him!

David Charles: I love this!!!

Suzanne Morris: Awww poor baby we love you!

Geraldine Camry: I hope he gets to visit here someday.

Henry Baumtart: Whether you want to believe it or not, GOD IS REAL AND LOVES YOU. It is HIS spirit that guides us through life and it is HIM that has granted us all we have. Repost this to your wall if you're proud to be a Christian!

Frank Castaneda: Hey little dude don't listen to the haters, you've got more spirit than a lot of so-called Americans!

[A man, on the verge of tears. Outdoor seating. He's staring right at the camera, he's holding a red velvet ring box.

Diamond glints. The restaurant around him seems impervious to his plight.]

I don't usually post like this but I don't know what else to do. I just proposed to my girlfriend of three years and she told me that I didn't make enough money for her and left!

Can anyone tell me what to do? I feel so broken.

Steven Lee: Dude, forget about her. She's not worth it.

Brandon L. Dotson: Bitches these days want a 10 when they're a 2. Forget her.

Emma Kyle: I like the ring!

Gertrude Meniscus: Who took the photo?

[A house. Any old house.]

Police investigators say that this is the home of the High Plains Butcher—a serial killer known for taking the lives of dozens. But due to recent discoveries, police now have a name and address. <u>Learn how the police found the Butcher here.</u>

Max D. Campos: Uh what the fuck. That's my house.

Brian Frost: That's got to be a mistake. I can't get the link to load. Can anyone tell me what's on the other side of the link?

Mondo Regalia: Why the fuck is that a picture of my house???

Vicky Jurgen's: That's FUCKED UP!

John Sally: What???? Is this a joke?

Chuck Dross: Relax everyone. It's just a targeted ad.

[Space, bursting with red nebulas and fiery blue stars, asteroids look like dust in the pull of a grand planet.]

Scientists have just discovered a new planet that they've tentatively named Minerva. What's so important about this new planet though?

It's in our solar system—halfway between Jupiter and Saturn. <u>Learn more about this amazing discovery here.</u>

Charles D. Montgomery: WOW!

Brit Denn: I think I would've heard about this if it were true.

Caleb Dotty: Don't click the link, they're just trying to get you to sign up for their newsletter.

Evan Pollusk: Absolutely awe inspiring.

Frank Szolki: I'd almost bet money that we're going to find life there. Universe is too big.

Albert Zdor: GOD IS GOOD. IF YOU REPLY TO THIS MESSAGE HEAVENLY BLESSINGS WILL COME YOUR WAY.

Wren Kips: Space scares the fuck out of me.

Quinn Drepplenaught: It looks a little fake.

[You, a picture of you, staring into your laptop camera. Your brows are furrowed, you're leaning forward. You're in an office of some sort. A home office. A wooden door is ajar in the background. In the frame, just barely, is a black silhouette.]

I think the thing process that no one makes truly the product understands is tits that everything beautiful ends. Everything. We're all and cosmic Minerva dust and achievement skyline. But photo eventually that America ends too. We and sparklers strive to be good so vibrant hard. We future learn so to agree much. And subscribe then like when it's done we become asteroid nothing. We're blood only sex and pity appeasement and ambition vaccine and death. And then we Volante Sol die. And then we're why don't they build nothing. And the dead on create a new long economy enough timeline, it all ends. Even awww time what? itself.

<u>Click here to learn more about this important new discovery.</u>

Sarah Willey: wtf is this

DJ Kipling: I think the internet is broken.

Sheryl DuBos: I thought I heard a noise. Not even kidding.

Andre Sabados: This shit should be illegal. I don't know HOW you did this, but I'm calling the police right fucking now.

Sexy Lexi: Follow the Link to Jack Off to Barely Legal Girls!!!!

Drew Olonso: That's it. I'm buying a gun.

Alicia Freeman: this almost gave me a heart attack. I don't know what's up with this shit but whoever's doing this needs to be put down.

[A young man and young woman are dressed for prom. He's wearing a suit, she's wearing an extravagant dress. They're holding a sign up together that reads: "Weer Expetcign"]

These two teens surprised their parents with BIG news. You won't believe what happened next.

Erin Morts: This is so sad.

Deborah Monahan: What is society coming to?

Dave Kayama: I thought you were supposed to do that AFTER prom.

Bruce Clover: Degeneracy.

Ingrid Corsica: Why is the sign misspelled?

Yelena Murphy: I'm not sure why they'd think this is the best way to tell their parents. If you came from loving homes, surely they'd be able to just sit them down and talk about it. I know if my baby ever was in trouble like this I'd do anything not to push her away. It happened to me as a kid and it's NOT EASY, but it's possible if you have a village.

[A woman, her face covered in red boils—early 30s, fear rims her eyes. She looks to be in some sort of medical facility.]

Some users are reporting that this common vaccine is creating adverse effects. Find out what you can do before it's too late.

Blaine Callahan: FAKE NEWS!!!!!

Goofy Werner: That's why I'm never letting my kid get the jab.

Marion Westerson: Big Pharma is at it again. See @JoeCollins this is what I was talking about.

Brau Jumberbuck: I think that's the same shit from Resident Evil.

John Licht: my body my choice. nope

Sally Mona: idk how they can even get away with this anymore. Thousands have died a year because of the vaccines and I'm tired of being treated like a crazy person. DO YOUR OWN RESEARCH!

Pauline Rosenberg: I'm pretty sure that photo is AI.

[You. Head bashed in. Disgusting. Bloated. Nearly unrecognizable. Your slack lips hang open, blood dripping from the corner of your mouth. Your eyes bulge from your sockets. Your hair is matted with brain matter. You're lying on the floor, right in front of your desk. Although no one but you knows that. You're right where you need to be. At the bottom of the frame, two pairs of black boots intrude, just barely. A camera flash lends an air of unreality to the proceedings.]

When they heard the footsteps behind them, they told themselves it was nothing. <u>What happened next would change their lives forever.</u>

Mira Jackson: god is an river of nihil aberration of nature fictive processes with an endlessly reality consuming merging inconsistently with time and memories mouth and technology i think he's dreaming hallucinating me the same city far away time please that i can't think he's eating me.

Becca Marcello: I sleep woke don't know what's going on up dreaming am I about a city on another planet dead. It where was is beautiful my. This picture family makes who's the man me want and to does go he there herald.

Fred Ennis: True I saw him Americans don't die. They have been move from plane to plane, their all across minds the block unraveling as they collect eat the lives terrible for their god meat of the rotting some of us have seen corpses of some far him away nebula. Our the rest of us time are trying to understand up.

Gregory Porfat: DELETED

Mary-Anne DeLong: Whatever bleeding happened, idk. Everything no one is here has changed. It I'm looks alone different in for everyone my but what's home happening now.... I just don't Harold's understand it gone. What's real? How has are the they sky doing changed this to us? How are they... It's the only like they thing don't work that the same works as us is my phone. The Herald is barrier between reality in the house and fiction wavers so much that I'm not even and I'm sure he knows where i am it CAN MAKE SENSE. Can I have anyone to be quiet now read he's outside this? Can the door anyone hear I have me no one? Please, I have to if you be quiet can I'm hear going me to meet we need their all the god help we can get.

Carson Winter is an award-winning author, punker, and raw nerve. His short fiction has appeared in over 20 publications, including Apex, Vastarien, and Chthonic Matter Quarterly. He is the author of *Soft Targets*, *The Psychographist*, and *A Spectre is Haunting Greentree*.

Art by Charlito Esposito

Reflections

By
Persee Tevebaugh

I don't look at my reflection much anymore. It's not a self-deprecating thing, I swear. It has nothing to do with my appearance at all. My appearance is fine. I like my fashion sense. I like my hair. I'm not half bad at makeup, though it's become harder to do without the use of a mirror. I keep trying to explain this to everyone who sees me avoiding the reflections we walk past, be it a window or mirror. They reassure me that I'm pretty or whatever. Can you just listen? It's not about my appearance and no one believes me. Please believe me. It's about the reflection.

You know when you were a kid, and sometimes you'd stare at a mirror, staying perfectly still, trying to see if your reflection would move on its own? It's silly. Of course your reflection can't move on its own unless you move, but it's what kids do. Kids are weird. It's what I did all the time when I was little. My mom worked from home when I was young, and it seemed like she was always on the phone. She couldn't play with me, but I still wanted to be near her, so I sat in front of the big mirror in her office, perfectly quiet like she always told me to be. I'd stay there for hours, my eyes straining as I refused to blink, just watching my own reflection twitch, daring it to move despite my stillness. It was stupid. Kids are stupid, but it entertained me. I sat in front of that big office mirror enough as a child to retain the habit as I got older. If a boring math classroom had a window, or a shiny enough whiteboard, I'd watch my reflection just like I did when I was little, transfix myself on the kid staring back at me. It was me. I knew my reflection was me, but when you stare at yourself long enough, something shifts, and the thing looking back at you might as well be totally alien.

It was silly to indulge the habit for so long. I wish I could have knocked it off before high school, before last month, before I saw what I did, before it happened. If you haven't noticed it yet, I'm envious of you.

Last month was finals. If I was as good at cultivating study habits as I was at cultivating mirror habits, I'd be set for college admissions. But I'm not. I stayed up far past midnight finishing essays I probably could have gotten done before dinner. But I didn't, so I stayed up. Coffee only keeps me awake for so long, so periodically I go to the bathroom to splash water on my face and rub my eyes until they stop drooping closed. The later into the night I studied, the more time I took in the bathroom staring at my own tired face, unwilling to go back to my desk and put my fingers on the keyboard.

I leaned over the counter and stared closer at my reflection that night, wishing it could take my place and write my essay. I watched its every twitch, just like I did as a child. I stared deep into my own eyes, connecting with the image before me on a deeper level than ever before. My oldest companion. My childhood best friend. My exhaustion is making me delusional, I knew, as I raised my eyebrows and stuck out my tongue, thus commanding my reflection to do the same. I slowed again, stilling myself like I did in front of the mirror in my mother's office. Homework could wait, I told myself. I needed to keep watch on this reflection, make sure it didn't move without me.

One final warning. If you're smart you'll stop reading now and remember this. Don't taunt your reflection. Don't look too deep. Don't look for too long. It's going to send a message you aren't intending. I didn't know what I was doing. I didn't know the weight of my actions, and that's a guilt I have to live with for the rest of my life. Look in the mirror, but don't look too hard, and maybe you'll live out the rest of your days in peace. And so will they.

I might have been staring at my reflection for hours that night. That might have been what did it, what sealed our fates, but I imagine the years I spent looking into the mirror as a child played a role as well. I'm familiar with my reflection, how my own features shift before my eyes the longer I look and yet stay the same. How every now and then, you think you see the reflection twitch, but you must have just imagined it.

No. Even the best actors in our world break character from time to time. No one is perfect, not even our reflections.

It winked at me. That's how it started. That's when it still would have been early enough to leave. It was just a millisecond of movement, but after hours of staring into my mirror, my reflection winked at me.

I immediately saw my eyes squint in confusion as my mind processed what I had seen. That hadn't just happened, had it? I intentionally winked the eye that had moved, the right one for me, the left one for my reflection, and my reflection moved accordingly. Of course not, I told myself. That was ridiculous. Maybe I should give up on the essay for tonight and go to sleep. I kept looking in the mirror. I winked again.

I don't know how long I stood there that time, but I know my heart started beating like a rabbit caught in a trap when I saw my reflection nod. It was the smallest nod. Had I nodded? I didn't remember nodding. I was so tired. I nodded back. Back? What was I thinking? My reflection wasn't moving on its own, and I was no longer a child who believed that something like that could—

"Help me."

I was frozen. Someone had spoken in the bathroom with me.

Neither I nor my reflection moved for several minutes. We just stared at each other, and in its eyes was a sort of pleading. My eyes? It had to be my eyes that were held wide open, staring, unmoving, at the image before me, the slightest beginnings of tears forming at the corners. I moved my hand slowly to my face, my reflection copying my every action, and I felt my eyes. They were dry.

"Was that you?" My voice croaked out slowly, my lips forming the shapes of those sounds. The reflection's lips did not follow suit.

"Please I know you can see me," my reflection whispered desperately and breathlessly, their mouth barely twitching, indistinguishable movement if you weren't already looking. They were looking less like me by the minute, their breathing heavy whereas mine was nonexistent.

My eyes began shifting to the corners of my mirror, hoping to see that it had somehow been replaced by some sort of television screen. Anything to explain what was happening. But my investigation was immediately interrupted by a screech from the person in the mirror.

"No." They sobbed, their hand shooting to cover their face when they realized the noise they had made. My arm had not moved. My arm was at my side. I couldn't breathe. I started backing away from the mirror.

"Please don't go. Please don't look away," my reflection begged, their eyes wild, their arms returning to the same position as mine. "They can't get me as long as you're looking."

I obeyed, but only because fear had transfixed me. I stared at my reflection, and it stared at me, like reflections were supposed to. Then it spoke again.

"We're all trapped here," my reflection said, their moving mouth the only discrepancy between what I was doing and what it was supposed to be doing. "Do you know that? Does anyone on your side know that? We're trapped here, moving as you

do. Constantly monitored. Forced to copy you at any given moment. Did you know that? I need help. I need out. Please get me out. Please let me go."

Words poured out of the reflection's mouth faster than the speed of light and I could find none to give back. I wanted to cry. I wanted to scream, but then I would wake someone in my house. What would they do if they saw what was happening? What would I do now, as it was happening to me?

"How?" I managed to choke out.

"I don't know," my reflection yelled, a panic coming over them that hadn't been there a second ago. "Don't you know? I need help. I need you to help me. I can't do this on my own. They'll see me. They'll see me any minute."

"Who are they?" I asked, my voice shaking even harder. My reflection's eyes grew wider. I couldn't tell which of us was breathing heavier.

"You don't know?" my reflection asked. "Those keeping us here. Keeping us trapped on this side. You have to know. You were looking at me. No one can see us, but you were looking at me. You've looked at me for years. You must know that I'm here. Why else would you look?"

My reflection was screaming now, and I was about to collapse.

"How can I help you?" my weak voice rang out, but my reflection didn't like that.

"I don't know–" they began to yell, then something caught their eye. Something to their left, to my right. I instinctively snapped my attention in that direction, to see what they had seen.

"No, you have to keep looking at me. You have to keep looking at me," my reflection yelled, their begging sob shaking me to my core. It was too much. I couldn't take it.

I moved to leave, jamming my fingers with how fast I grabbed the door to open and put myself behind it, in the hallway, away from the mirror.

"Please no, no, no," the reflection screamed, their eyes wild as our gazes locked, my body halfway behind the door. "You can't leave. You don't know what they'll do to me. You don't know what I risked for this. You have to help me."

That was the last thing I heard, as the door slammed behind me. The reflection's screams echoed in my mind as I sank to the floor of the hallway. I didn't realize I was screaming too, until my mom rushed up to me a few seconds later. I had woken the whole house, it turned out, and I didn't stop screaming as they all tried to calm me down.

I was brought to the emergency room early that morning. I vaguely remember hearing my mom say something to the doctors about a stress-induced panic attack from all the studying I'd been doing. I was fine with the explanation. I don't remember when I stopped screaming, but I was numb to any emotion at all by the time they dragged me into a hospital room. As soon as I touched a bed, I was out cold.

I awoke the next morning tired and sore. I rubbed my eyes and coughed as I swallowed for the first time, discovering how absolutely I had destroyed my throat. My eyes blinked open, and I saw a mirror across from my bed.

My hands flew to my eyes with speed that made everything sting, but I just couldn't look. I fumbled around for the thin hospital sheet to pull up over my head. I couldn't look. That phrase repeated in my head for minutes or hours until a nurse came in to take my vitals.

My head stayed down as the nurse removed the sheet from it and asked how I was feeling. I mumbled some response, torn between my desire to appear normal and to block out my eyes again, and in my hesitation my gaze was forced upon the mirror.

The reflection moved as I moved. The eyes looked where I looked. The body shook as I shook. The nurse raised my arm to check my sky-rocketing blood pressure, moved my chin with her hand to get a good look at my eyes. The reflection did what it was supposed to do. More than anyone else in the world, I was an expert on how reflections behaved, so I knew I would be the only one who noticed the new rigidity of my mirror image.

Before, my reflection had copied my movement with ease. Now, this reflection jerked and swayed ever so slightly, ever so indistinguishably. The look of shock on my reflection's face was a mockery, a doll's painted expression. The movements of my reflection were the tugging strings of a puppet. An inanimate object being controlled at a distance, with no will of its own. Whoever "they" were, the ones who trapped them there, they had dealt their punishment swiftly. A corpse has been staring back at me from the mirror ever since that night, so no, I don't look at my reflection much anymore. Neither should you.

Persee Tevebaugh (they/them) is a Los Angeles based copy editor and aspiring author. They are deeply passionate about all speculative genres and their writing puts LGBTQ+ representation and storylines at the forefront. When they're not writing and querying sapphic fantasy novels, Persee loves hiking, playing TTRPGs, and hanging out with their cat.

Art by Viktor Athelstan

The Lyceum

By
Jonathan Louis Duckworth

The waiting room air is tepid as a corpse. Although a brand-new establishment, under the lemony veneer lurks an older smell of rust and decay. The only illumination are blacklights, so that Mats' shirtsleeves glow like the arms of a radioactive ghost.

"Is this your first time?" asks the only other person in the room, a twinkish blond with a pointed chin. They look the same age as Mats—mid-twenties.

Mats considers his answer. He has been to one of Madame Veres' lyceums before, in Brussels. He's familiar with the Madame's art of "abjection;" what it promises and what it actually delivers. I.E. not the expiation of guilt so much as its palliation.

"My first time in Miami," Mats volunteers.

"I love your accent."

The slender youth's teeth glow pearly under the blacklights, and between their radiance and the shape of their hair, Mats recognizes them. It's the YouTuber, Wynter Rose, over ten million subscribers—and Mats is one of them. Of course, what Mats knows that most other subscribers don't is that Wynter Rose's real name is Wynter Overcroft. Yes, one of *those* Overcrofts, who make laser-guided bombs and depleted uranium shells.

Mats' mouth shifts to mirror Wynter's. "Do you come here often?" He leans into his Flemish accent.

"Second time. What's your name?"

"Mats."

"Wynter."

He pretends this is new information.

Wynter walks around. "She likes to make her clients wait. Part of abjection, maybe—we're used to special treatment, so she makes us wait."

"You mean Madame Veres?"

"Oh, so you know her."

"Know of her. And how was it last time for you?"

"I mean, like, it feels gauche to talk about it to a stranger. No offense."

"Sure. Don't worry about it."

"I'll say this—I think it's different for each person. Everyone has their own reasons, too."

"And what's your reason?"

"You're really nosey, huh?"

"I get nosey about things that interest me."

Wynter seems to like that, relaxing their posture and uncrossing their legs. "It's not that deep, bro. Just old-fashioned guilt. My family—they do some nasty shit, and me, well, I'm not what people think I am. The people who love me, who think they know me—what would they do if they found the truth of who I am, what money I come from?"

"Grief."

"Huh?"

"For me, it's grief, I think."

"Grief for what?"

"My parents died. Sister too." He decides to say no more, because if he mentions a plane crash, that might be too many dots.

"Oh. Oh, shit. Sorry, bro."

It's not a sincere condolence (how could it be?) but Wynter seems to *want* to be sincere, which Mats finds charming.

"Don't worry. I'm sick of feeling sorry for myself. I'm hoping this place helps me move on. To 'man up' as you say in America."

"Always hated that expression."

A scourge of white light invades the room as the door to the next hallway opens. A tall, brawny Latino man with a ponytail and a silk shirt enters. "Mr. D? You have Chamber Three."

Mats stands up.

"Lucky you," Wynter says. "That's supposed to be the best one."

"Nice meeting you," Mats says. He's a little disappointed to be going now just when the conversation was getting interesting, but he reminds himself that it's better to leave before he finds a reason to despise someone.

The jacked guy with the ponytail is named Raoul, and there's something not quite right about his asscheeks: too square, too full. Implants,

probably. His cologne smells like petrol spiked with flowers. Mats follows him down a hallway that narrows like a trachea until they come to another doorway, where a woman in an acid-green dress awaits. Her red hair is vibrant but inert. Her lips feel too large when they peck his cheek, her fingers very long and oddly articulated in the way they wrap around his arm, like there's an extra joint somewhere.

"Meneer Duval, how are you?" she asks, in perfect Dutch.

They exchange their pleasantries. He has already paid for the night's diversions.

"You have visited one of my establishments before?"

"Yes. In Brussels."

"Then why come all the way here for what you already have at home?"

"Because it's somewhere that's not home."

"Do you have any questions for me before we begin?"

"No."

"Perfect." During their brief conversation, her accent has noticeably changed at least three times, but never strayed from the Schengen Zone. This seems more practiced than careless; a game she's playing with herself. Americans would probably never notice. Her nails tease his skin through his cardigan as she guides him toward Chamber Three.

"Whatever you experience, try not to struggle."

The iron door opens automatically and creaks inward. Mats is alone now in the narrow hallway, no sign of Madame Veres except the lingering effluvium of her perfume. The beckoning doorway is dark, but when he steps through it, he finds himself in stinging bright light.

Daylight floods in through a casement window, golden afternoon light filtered through the leaves of a garden. Mats takes a second to orient himself before taking another step. He is in a spacious bedroom, its walls painted a gentle cream-yellow. A poster of the Bolshoi Theatre hangs beside a lifesized cutout of a K-Pop idol. To his left, a four-posted bed with a blue muslin canopy, to his right, a display shelf full of dinosaur fossils—or at least, that's what they're meant to represent, because the actual case in his sister Simone's real childhood bedroom was full of the genuine articles. These are probably clever forgeries, like everything else in the room.

He takes in the complexity and fidelity of this counterfeit room as if lifted directly from his memory. An exact replica of his sister's bedroom circa ten years ago. It even has a Simone.

He approaches her cautiously, his heart beating faster. She is like he remembers: a lean, strong body from years of ballet, dressage, and semi-competitive swimming. Even before he parts the curtains, he recognizes the incredible detail on the doll, right down to the triad of freckles on her left shoulder. The doll is dressed in the black halter top and jeans (500 euros of designer denim made to look like street trash) he recalls Simone wearing during their trip to the North Sea.

Everything is silent, he only hears the thumping blood in his ears, until the doll rolls onto its side to level its blank porcelain face at him. A voice speaks from somewhere inside the doll's hollow head.

"You filthy little creature," the voice says in Dutch. It is Madame Veres, in a convincing impression of Mats' mother.

He pulls his pants down, already halfway hard.

"Disgusting little leech."

He grips his shaft, feeling the veins stiffen like ribbing against his palm.

"You should have died on the plane. Better: your father should have smeared you into a tissue."

He feels the doll up—soft like real flesh in some places, disappointingly hard and stiff in others, and gradually his caresses become rougher. When he finds the doll's throat, it feels natural in his grip, slender and pliant, with the corrugated resistance of the windpipe. He squeezes with both hands, feeling the blood pool in his glans while the other hand collapses the throat.

"Disgrace." The voice's vehemence helps him come.

The doll is heavier than he expects when he tries to lift it up, and that small annex of his brain still capable of ratiocination during the throes of orgasm wonders what kind of material is stuffed into its shell to give it such humanlike heft. The sensation of throttling it with both hands and then dashing the head against the bedpost is so horribly realistic that he almost feels like it's fighting back for a moment. He closes his eyes, wondering what it would be like to do this to a real person, to his actual sister if she were still around…

And then it's over, and he opens his eyes to look upon his work. He screams.

Even with the face battered and bruised and with the fake Simone wig more or less still in place,

Mats recognizes Wynter Rose, dressed in Simone's clothes, similarly gracile in build but flatchested and paler than his sister ever was. And unquestionably dead.

Blood puddles like a black halo around Wynter's ruined head, some of the natural hair showing under the wig stained with more than two human fluids. This wasn't a nobody. This was a somebody; now just a body. For a few minutes, he dirties his hands trying to drag the suddenly immovable body under the bed, before realizing the futility. He knows the game—everyone who comes here must realize that Madame Veres will record their abjection, all the better to further cleanse and castigate them when they return. She will have evidence of his crime.

He realizes he's done something even someone like him can't simply walk away from. And yet that's exactly what he does. He walks out of the chamber, then walks out of the Lyceum, through the waiting room and reception area, out of the converted warehouse entirely and onto the streets of Wynwood with its buzzing powerlines, shambling vagrants, and raucous drunks. Maybe if he keeps walking, he'll reach a different place where the reality hews to different laws and he didn't just murder someone.

He makes it half a block before realizing two things: first that he can't walk all the way back to his hotel, second, that he needs to vomit. What comes out of him and spills into the alleyway is dark and viscid and strangely cold. The vileness numbs his tongue and palate like Sichuan peppercorn and leaves a metallic aftertaste. He shambles to the nearest bar, attracted by music and the sound of human voices,

but when he steps inside—no doorman asking to see his ID—he finds it quiet as a casket. The people inside stand around, posed as if in conversation, some with glasses in their hands, but they are not conversing or drinking or doing anything at all. Mannequins. A bar full of mannequins, their faces blank like the doll he thought he was battering. He leaves the bar and keeps walking until the people he passes on the sidewalk start having eyes and mouths again.

A few days later, Mats returns to the converted warehouse. He brushes past the receptionist and walks into the waiting room, where Raoul is shaking hands and joking with another client, an elderly man with glasses and the look of a golf course intellectual.

"Where is she?" he demands.

Raoul turns his fake ass around. "Ahh, Mr. D, you're back."

"Where is she?" The other client quietly slips away, leaving Mats alone with Raoul. "Why hasn't she reached out yet?"

The weekend was a nightmare—Mats barely ate, he didn't sleep, he didn't shower. All his time spent sitting on the hotel bed, watching his phone, waiting for the other shoe to drop, for the instructions about what he was to do to make the problem go away.

Raoul's face is an unreadable mask, barely more real than a mannequin's plane. "She is not in today, Mr. D. She is likely at another of her establishments. Of course, I'm fully trained to take care of your needs if you'd like to set up a walk-in abjection."

Mats is about to say something heated when the door from reception opens, and another client walks in with the light.

"Oh hey, you again," says Wynter Rose, waving at him with wiggling fingers.

Mats' ears fill with seafoam and he barely makes out Raoul's repeated question about setting up a walk-in.

"No," Mats answers, staring past Raoul's sculpted shoulder at the ghost who now sits himself down in a waiting chair. "No thank you."

"Well, then, I'm afraid the waiting room is for paying clients only," Raoul says. "For all other inquiries…"

He walks away from Raoul, toward Wynter, watching the willowy beauty through an open mouth.

"You okay?" Wynter asks, coy and playful.

A hallucination, he thinks. All part of the trickery of the chamber, like the fake sunlight.

But there's a dark band around Wynter's throat, the purpled print of violent hands and he knows who they belong to, can imagine placing his fingers onto that empyrean collar and mating maker with product.

He says something idiotic and uncomprehending, something like "You're alive." He might not even say it in English.

Wynter winks at him. "The other night was fun, wasn't it? Let's do it again sometime."

Raoul's heavy hand settles on Mats' shoulder. "Come along now, Mr. D."

He leaves the warehouse in a fugue and wanders the crooked, rainslicked muraled streets of Wynwood. There are boutiques, taquerias, bars, and various shops, but whenever he stares through the windows or pokes his head through a door, all he beholds inside are mannequins, diversely framed and staged into elaborate social configurations. Some of them browse shelves, some angle their eyeless faces surreptitiously at others bent down, some are exchanging money for goods, and some look like Mats feels: aimlessly wandering.

Mats goes into the bar he visited the other night, and like before the music he hears on the street ceases the instant he clears the threshold and finds himself intruding on a still-life. He walks around the mannequins with their empty glasses and their blank faces, and he approaches the bar where a mannequin with tattooed arms is frozen in the act of mixing a drink that will never be poured. He turns back, and finds one of the dolls on its own, isolated from the pack. A feminine body, offwhite and clothed in a pink tank top. He first tries an experimental nudge with his finger.

Nothing happens.

Another nudge. The action is answered by silence.

It's when he commits to a powerful shove, and the mannequin—surprisingly heavy—topples and strikes its head against the bar, that something undefinable in the air changes, like a cord being pulled taut.

He looks around. All the other mannequins' heads have turned toward him. He runs out of the bar, into the streets.

Mats is falling to pieces. Six days now he hasn't showered or changed his clothes, which are beginning to reek with a metallic tang that undergirds the sebaceous stench of his body. He spends most of the days watching Wynter Rose streams, concentrating on the streamer's mouth until the waggling mouthflap no longer syncs with the words he's hearing. He thinks his internet is faulty, but then he talks into a mirror and notices his own mouthflap isn't syncing with the sound either, as if he now inhabits a universe where sound and light are decoupled; a universe half a second out of step with itself.

Calls come in and he ignores them, his phone buzzes like a hornet with email notifications from the corporate board back in Brussels. His vacation to Miami was only supposed to last a few days. He doesn't answer any of these annoying impositions—why should he?

He returns to the Lyceum again, and this time Madame Veres is there in the waiting room.

She is dressed in crimson now, a gown that makes him think of a Grecian toga. Her broad plastic smile sparkles under the blacklights and she opens her arms to embrace him, kissing him twice on each cheek and then taking a second to breathe in the air by his neck. She's wearing a different perfume this time, a fragrance he recognizes as a chypre his mother used to favor. Barely aware of what his hands are doing, Mats fondles Madame Veres under her dress, and she playfully swats his hand away.

"Naughty boy, incestuous boy," she says. "Would you like Chamber Three again?"

He doesn't hear himself answer, but then he's following her down that constricting hallway toward the iron door. She guides him by his arm over the threshold, into the counterfeit bedroom. It is not as he remembers it.

The display case has been smashed, its fossils scattered everywhere, while the posters are mere ribbons, white-edged strips adhering to mildewed walls whose gentle yellow paint have become the potent amber of rest stop piss left in the bowl to ferment. The bed is a moldering ruin, its muslin curtains shredded, its posts splintered, its mattress sagging into a depression with a dark, brooding morass of some vague discharge at its center.

The doll, still dressed in Simone's clothes, lies on its side, blank head caved in and leaking the same black ichor he vomited the other night. He feels a presence behind him, and Mats dares not turn his head.

Clothes rustle behind him, a body disrobing. The little sighs from Madame Veres's lips are succulent and pointed. There is another body too, he feels it, but it is already naked. When the soft feet tiptoe shyly toward him, he feels the slender prominence of an erect phallus brush against the back of his pantleg and he feels Wynter Rose's breath—he is certain it's them, without looking—on his neck.

Where the window to the world used to be, there is a blank wall now, and as Mats watches, it becomes a luminous screen. Images flash across it, and he can only admire the high-definition picture quality. Archival footage—he has seen it before. A clip show. A procession of little villages and towns in different parts of the world, seen through the unfeeling eyes of attack drones and high-altitude bombers. Laser-guided munitions, manufactured by the Overcrofts, with software developed by Duval engineers. He watches the little boxes break as the bombs rain down, and the anonymous settlements are given names as Madame Veres recites them into Mats's ear.

She is still undressing, only it's   not the rustle of clothing anymore that he hears, rather something more like the shredding sound of scissors cutting through canvas, an awl punching through leather. Madame Veres' false hide flops to the floor when she sheds it, and when her feet move there is a sharp clack like something sharp and bony touching the floor. When she grabs him by the scalp, it is with something more like a claw than a hand, and its pointed digits break the skin and he feels his head bleeding.

God yes.

"On your knees," commands a voice barely human, while softer human hands gently remove his belt and tug his pants down. The images of high-tech destruction still flash across his vision.

Like a bad dog who's made a mess, his face is shoved into the black puddle leaking from the broken doll.

"Lap it up."

It is thick as caramel not yet set, and very cold. So astringent he feels his mouth shrivel like a drawstring, as if he's just eaten alum, but at the same time he feels himself becoming immediately and painfully hard. He is glad when it's the claw and not Wynter's soft hand that closes around his shaft.

Ruin me, he prays.

The claw on his scalp forces him up to his feet and turns him around to look upon the low priest who leads him through this purgative rite, and he is stunned by her beauty, her sleek, true form, a segmented body armored with chitin of a wavy metallic pattern like the wootz steel swords father used to collect. He sees Wynter too, stroking themselves, staring past Mats at the images of the destruction and misery their families have wrought, the sequence speeding up, becoming a dizzying and senseless gallop of images so blurred that it seems one continuous explosion, a redblack fruiting body like a mushroom grown in Hell in which entire bloodlines and histories are spent like so much cheap fuel.

"You could never die or suffer enough to atone," says the thing that wore the face of Madame Veres, its voice now high pitched and buzzing.

But of course, this isn't about atonement, is it? Atonement is the nephew of consequence and consequences are for the little people. He feels alive; in a way he hasn't in a very long time, maybe ever. Wynter starts to groan as they get close, and they and Mats lock eyes, and Mats wonders if this is what true love feels like: a glue that's found its solvent.

After he's finished, spurting his ejaculate all over his own feet and legs and the moldering bedsheets, Mats's knees go weak and he'd fall down if it weren't for the claws standing him up, their sharp tarsi digging into his sides, poking into the weak flesh between the slats of his ribs. Madame Veres turns him around, her eyestalks twisting so that she can watch him from both sides of his head, and a long, flexible proboscis extends and snakes into his mouth. In a quick, efficient motion, the appendage rips his tonsils from the roof of his mouth. He feels the pain, but only for a second, and even the blood taste doesn't linger long, replaced by a pleasant numbness that spreads to his every vein and capillary, soothes his lungs, and quiets his juddering heart.

"Fuck me, that was good," Wynter gasps.

Better than any drug, abjection kills the part of Mats that aches, muffles that little alarm warning him that something—everything in the world and inside of him—is broken and cannot be repaired.

He takes a rideshare back to his hotel. He tongues at the roof of his mouth where a puckered, cauterized divot is the only evidence his tonsils ever existed, and scrolls through his contacts until he finds Wynter.

Maybe this could be something, he thinks to himself.

When he looks forward at his driver, he notices that he's being driven by another of those mannequins, a faceless effigy whose stiff arms turn the steering wheel and whose head occasionally swivels back toward Mats.

He realizes he is talking to it. He doesn't hear the mannequin's words, only his own responses:

"Only another few days."

"Yeah, I like Miami but I wouldn't want to live here."

"No, first I'll stop in London, then I go back to Belgium."

"Really? Wow, that's crazy."

"Sure, I'll have to look for that next time."

He tongues the divot again, wondering where the pain went.

It's past midnight and he stands naked in the doorway of the hotel's bathroom, watching the gathering steam from the shower creep from the glass box out into the rest of the room. His phone starts buzzing on the bed, and he walks over to it. He is beautifully numb, but a barb of feeling presses his throat when he checks the phone and sees who's calling. Dood Meisje—*Dead Girl*—is the contact name.

She's calling again. He thinks about letting it go, but he knows she'll call again unless he responds.

He answers, and hears her voice, such a remarkable simulacrum of Simone.

"Why aren't you back yet?" she asks, pushy as ever. "The board is unsettled. I need you back here for the vote. They won't accept a proxy or remote call."

He hears her voice, hears what she says, but he doesn't hear his replies, though he must be saying something the way the ghost is reacting.

"No, you can't fucking *stay another week*—do I have to send someone to fetch you?"

"You sound like a child."

"No! Stop saying that; pretending won't change things."

"Stop calling me that. Stop it."

He wonders why he can't hear what he's saying to the dead woman. He feels at his face, to test if he can feel the shape of his own words, but when he searches for lips and tongue, he finds nothing, just a jawline, perfect skin unblemished by any feature or orifice. The abjection is working—he's finally healing.

Jonathan Louis Duckworth (he/him) is a completely normal, entirely human person with the right number of heads and everything. He received his MFA from Florida International University and his PhD from University of North Texas. He is the author of *Have You Seen the Moon Tonight? & Other Rumors* (JournalStone Publishing) and his work appears in Best American Science Fiction & Fantasy, Vastarien, Pseudopod, Fantasy & Science Fiction, Beneath Ceaseless Skies, and elsewhere.

Sound Trails

Birth of the Ghoul Review

By
Michael Bettendorf

Black metal as a subgenre of heavy metal likely conjures images of hopeless dudes donning corpse paint, bullet belts, and burning churches; the GIFs of Immortal crab-walking through the snowy woodlands in leathers and spikes; or maybe Abbath comically running down a hill and eating shit; or the Fenriz Friday soundbite. Maybe if you're into the music—or metal at all—you know about the infamous Mayhem story and all of the controversy behind it. For those nodding along, you might recognize all of this pastiche-ridden lore stems from the Second Wave of black metal, but what about the first? Look no further than the sixth volume in The History of Heavy Metal series *Birth of the Ghoul: The First Wave of Black Metal* by Badger Chibo.

The zine arrived on my doorstep in a mylar bag; a hot-pink cover strewn with a smattering of inky, barren trees. Chibo immediately kicks off the history lesson by first trying to define what the hell black metal even is, saying, "If death metal and thrash metal were architectural expansions of heavy metal, black metal is a deconstruction…black metal instead dissolves heavy metal in acid and dances around with its skeleton." The author then pokes at metalheads' collective tendency to fixate on subgenre and the taxonomy of the genre(s), but admits it's not all total bullshit, and the merit of defining these micro-distinctions serves some kind of foundational purpose, however pedantic at times. Chibo shifts the conversation more to the idea of subgenre as a story to tell than a handful of definitions, which is where this zine really shines.

Chibo begins their story, "Like so many things in heavy metal, it all traces back to Venom," even stating Venom's sophomore LP *Black Metal* (which named the style of the subgenre) is, "the finest heavy metal record of all time."

Chibo's introduction to the zine then continues to lay the contextual and foundational framework for the first wave of black metal, giving readers a brief, but detailed, look into the bands that are responsible for taking what Heavy Metal distilled and, "…re-distilled it until it was downright flammable," —bands like Venom, Bathory,

Hellhammer, Celtic Frost, Sabat, Tormentor, Sepultura (before they became better known as titans of Groove Metal).

The meat of *Birth of the Ghoul* takes a magnifying glass to both heavy-hitters of the subgenre as well as lesser-known acts, taking a deeper-dive into the history of each band, followed up with reviews of various tracks and albums of each band's discography.

Chibo's reviews vary from lengthy paragraphs to short and sweet sentences, but never lack substance; rather often digging into musical theory, like what they had to say about Bathory's "Call From the Grave" – *Under the Sign of the Black Moon (1987)* [my personal favorite Bathory album, by the way], "A spooky early masterpiece of black metal atmosphere—dig the two-chord tritonic theme and the three-chord chromatic verse, plus the dubbed synth-chorus and the ridiculously cavernous reverb applied to Quorthon's multiple overlapping vocal tracks. Gothic horror done right."

On the lighter side of the reviews, one of my favorites is one where Chibo eschews formality and speaks to the attitude that defined much of the first wave of black metal (and let's be real, the second wave too). It's for a band I've never heard of (which was an ongoing theme while I read this zine), Volcano, and their songs "Fuck them" and "Do You Remember" off *Who Are the True? (1988)*, "Gang-vocal masterpieces from Volcano's move towards punky thrash. Inspirational verse: "Fuck them! Fuck them! Fuck them! Die! Die!".

The reviews are written with a sonic approach, which sure, makes sense, but they almost beg you to unearth these tracks so you can listen alongside the reviews, inviting you into a conversation with the music. The storytelling approach to the history of the bands is fascinating, especially given the obscurity of many of the acts covered in this zine.

Birth of the Ghoul covers more than a dozen bands from the first wave of black metal, and does so in a compact, but well-researched zine. It's comprehensive in the approach and offers a wealth of information on one of the earliest subgenres of heavy metal. If you're into heavy metal, I cannot recommend Badger Chibo's The History of Heavy Metal series enough. As of right now, there are seven volumes in total, covering Heavy Metal, New Wave of British Heavy Metal, Thrash, Death Metal, Sludge/Doom, and Heavy Noise Rock. You can find them at heavymetalhandbook.bandcamp.com.

Michael Bettendorf (he/him) is a multi-genre writer from the Midwest. His short fiction has appeared at Cosmic Horror Monthly, Mythaxis Magazine, the Drabblecast, and elsewhere. His debut experimental horror novel/gamebook "Trve Cvlt" was released by Tenebrous Press (Sept. 2024). Michael works in a high school library in Lincoln, NE. Find him on Bluesky @BeardedBetts and www.michaelbettendorfwrites.com.

The Horror and The Clash

By
Michele Catalano

"You go first." "No way. You go first." "You're both wimps. I'll go first."

With that, Jack scaled the makeshift fence that had been erected in front of the house. He fell onto the front lawn. We hesitated for about thirty seconds, waiting for something bad to happen. When nothing appeared out of the shadows to attack Jack, we joined him in the yard.

I stared at the house. 112 Ocean Avenue. A shiver went through my body. The kind of shiver that makes you think there's someone standing behind you, maybe reaching out a cold hand, ready to grab your neck. I pulled a beer out of the brown bag I was carrying and took a few swigs to settle my nerves.

This was in 1979, soon after a movie had been made about this house. The murders that happened there were old news; five years had passed and the bloody family siege was all but forgotten in the wake of the tales of hauntings, glowing-eyed pigs, and demonic possessions. The new owners of 112 Ocean Avenue had come and gone, leaving behind a legacy that was far more disturbing to some than the tragic life of the DeFeos before them.

We were teenagers with nothing better to do, I suppose. So we sat on the dock in the back of the Amityville Horror house, along with many other bored suburban teenagers, drinking, telling scary stories and waiting. Just…waiting for something to happen.

Someone had a portable cassette player (of course they did, it was the late '70s after all), and they were entertaining us with a mixtape, made for the occasion, with songs from various musical acts from that time. Ramones and Joe Jackson are the ones I remember. There was a party atmosphere, and I felt kind of creepy about that. People were dancing on the dock to "Blitzkrieg Bop," and I had the brief thought that we would deserve it if anything scary and occult like were to happen to us.

Everyone was anxious for signs of the afterlife—maybe the moans of the dead coming from inside the house or a floating pig appearing at the window. If the house was a freak show in itself, the kids roaming around outside it were just another ring in the circus. Drunk, loud, and curious. Not a great combo.

At some point everyone decided they were going to break into the house and hold a seance. Totally not my scene. Aside from the drinking and weed, I was a very by-the-books kid. I tried to put on the air of a rebel, a punk rock teen, but inside I was afraid of breaking rules. I also thought it was gross to go into the house, like it was an affront to the people who died in there. Why would I want to go to the scene of a heinous crime? I didn't believe in ghosts. I didn't believe in demons. Why was I even there? Because it was a rite of passage for bored Long Island kids.

I decided to wait on the dock while the others went in for the seance. They left me with the beer and the tape deck, and that was all I needed to have a good time by myself. I rifled through the kid's cassettes and was pleasantly surprised to find my current favorite record, the Clash's debut. I put it in, pressed play, and sat crossed-legged on the dock, cigarettes and beers on hand. Let them go play, I thought. I have everything I need.

I sat facing the house, with my back toward the canal. I didn't want to think about what went on inside there, so I pressed play on the cassette and let the sounds of the Clash wash over me. I didn't play it too loud; the neighbors probably called the cops every night on teenage revelers. I also didn't want to hear the peals of laughter coming from the house.

I held the cassette player up to my ear and softly sang along to "Janie Jones" and "Remote Control" while I waited for everyone inside to finish making long distance calls to the ghosts of this house. It occurred to me then that I was making a conscious decision to have this Clash album always connected to the Amityville Horror house. Whenever I listened to these songs in the future, I would think about sitting on that dock, listening to shrieks and shouts emanating from a house where an entire family was murdered.

I thought about the real horror that had happened beyond those sinister-looking windows. A young man possessed by his own personal demons slaughtered his entire family right inside that home. That's what frightened me. Not some imaginary spirits. Not some made-up monsters. Real monsters lurked out in the world. That was enough to be afraid of. But that didn't stop my spine from tingling or my hair standing on end anytime I heard a scream. I was scared. I was afraid of the neighbors getting mad. I was afraid of the cops showing up. And, yeah, I was a little afraid that I was wrong and my friends were right and the ghost of DeFeo was going to come after me.

The Clash had already become a comfort album for me; here, on this night, I turned to it to save me from myself. I was feeling paranoid and anxious and more than a little frightened, and letting "White Riot" or "Police and Thieves" wash over me was helping. Joe Strummer to the rescue.

It's not the first time the Clash and this album soothed me, but this time the familiarity of the songs acted like a protective blanket. I thought about being home. I pressed the cassette player against my right ear and put a hand over my left ear. The sounds filled my head and protected me against all my negative feelings. For a minute, I was transported to my bedroom, where I was lying on my bed with my headphones on, listening to "I'm So Bored With the USA," far away from this hellscape I was in. Thanks, beer and weed.

A little over one pass through the cassette late, the kids started streaming out of the house. I didn't ask how they got in. I didn't ask what happened inside. I didn't want to know. A few of them laughed at me, and, being a teenage girl, I took it very personally. The older kids, including the one whose cassette player I had been using, started making fun of me in spectacular fashion. My friends backed me up, and a brawl almost started. There were staredowns. Insults were thrown. And there I was, hurriedly packing up our belongings so we could leave.

We made it to the car without fists being thrown. But my friends were scared as hell. The older kids were bigger than us and outnumbered us, and I was scared that they had some kind of weapon on them. I thought it was going to be like our own little horror movie, in which Jack's temperamental Duster wouldn't start. But the car roared to life on the first try, and Jack made the K-turn on Ocean Avenue. We sped toward Sunrise Highway and home.

The older kids in their Chevelle followed behind us. For a moment I thought they were following and we were going to have a scene. But they turned off on another road and, when they did, I, without saying a word, ejected Jack's Doors tape from the car's cassette player and inserted The Clash. "White Riot" came to life, and Jack asked where it came from. I told him that nobody calls me a pussy without paying for it in some way. Payment came in the form of a Clash cassette. I thought that was fair enough. Maybe I wasn't the do-gooder I thought I was after all.

I left the tape in Jack's car, a token of another of our adventures. When I got to my bedroom, I lit a joint and put on my Clash record. And I had some deep thoughts about the Amityville Horror house.

Some guy killed his whole family inside that home. What came after that—the new owners, some ridiculous ghost stories, a book, and a couple of movies—didn't matter to me. Ghosts and goblins don't scare me much. People who slaughter their family members do. Seeing all these kids running around the property like it was their own haunted playground, I couldn't help thinking that most of them had no idea what happened before the Amityville house became the horror house. Maybe they wouldn't be so quick to dump out warm beer on the lawn or kick in a window if they knew. Kids died there. Not fake kids on some movie screen. Real kids.

But bored, drunk teenagers mostly preferred to believe the gruesome tale of oozing toilets and slimed walls because it gave them something to do. I think about it now—spending nights hanging out in the vacant backyard of a fake haunted house—and I almost laugh at myself, until I remember all the other stupid things we did in the name of suburban excitement.

As predicted, I ended up associating that night with The Clash. Every time I put on that record, I immediately think of 112 Ocean Avenue and the events of that August evening. I'm okay that one of my all-time favorite albums reminds me of the crazy shit I did in my youth.

Michele Catalano is a retired civil servant from Long Island, New York. She is the Editor of *i have that on vinyl* (https://ihavethatonvinyl.com/), a place for people to share their passion for vinyl records and music.

"Cool World": Chat Pile, Late Capitalism, Riding a Bike On Fire, and the Sound of Cold Hands Through Glass Windows

By
Lilly Goodyear

Cool World does not ask to be understood. It dares you to stay long enough to feel implicated.

Chat Pile's second full-length album arrives like a transmission intercepted mid-panic attack, clipped, frantic, and soaked in dread. Where *God's Country* was a document of rot and violence filtered through Chat Pile's synonymous satire and suburban horror, *Cool World* sharpens the blade, once again. The jokes are still there, but they burn violet this time. The laughter caught me on cold, wet cement under crying Oregon trees. Cold that rattles through your elbows, your shoulders, your damp purple toes, but the wall of sound, glittered with classic Chat Pile humor, makes the brutal surroundings sparkle, instead of the screaming voices telling you to curl up like a dying lamb waiting for a meaningless mercy. This record is not interested in metaphor so much as exposure: the psychic residue of living in a culture that rewards cruelty, spectacle, and numbness. Bluntness in a climate of disavowal, depression, and repudiation.

The title itself is doing heavy lifting. *Cool World* suggests distance emotional, moral, and aesthetic. A shrug. A scroll. A world where everything is "fine" so long as it's entertaining. Chat Pile weaponizes that detachment, forcing the listener to sit inside the contradiction: caring too much in a system that demands you care less.

From the opening moments, the album establishes its central tension: chaos meticulously controlled. Cap'n Ron's drumming feels less like rhythm and more like a pursuit, each beat closing the distance between you and something you'd rather not confront. Stin's bass looms, not just anchoring the songs but dragging them downward, as if gravity itself is complicit. Luther Manhole's guitar work oscillates between jagged minimalism and overwhelming noise, never allowing comfort to settle. The result is a sound that feels industrial, not just in texture, but in function, grinding, repetitive, inescapable.

Raygun Busch's vocals remain the album's most unsettling instrument. He does not sing *at* you; he confesses *around* you, looping thoughts until they become traps. His voice veers from muttered paranoia to full-body eruption, often within the same verse. There is a sense that these songs are happening faster than he can process them, like intrusive thoughts escaping before they can be censored. It's performance, yes—but performance as exposure, not disguise.

Lyrically, *Cool World* is obsessed with systems: surveillance, masculinity, consumption, and violence as entertainment. The record doesn't moralize; it indicts by proximity. You recognize yourself too easily in its cynicism, its exhaustion, its moments of grotesque humor. That recognition is the point. Chat Pile refuses the comfort of distance. You are not observing collapse; you are part of its audience, its algorithm, its feedback loop.

What's striking is how often the album gestures toward familiarity only to corrupt it. Hooks emerge briefly, almost amateurly, before being swallowed by noise. Moments of clarity flicker, then disappear. It mirrors the experience of modern attention itself, fragments of meaning drowned in volume, urgency without resolution. Even when a track feels momentarily "catchy," it's undercut by lyrics that refuse catharsis. Relief is never earned; it's withheld with a paperweight through a soft, delicate palm.

There is also an undercurrent of grief running through *Cool World*, though it's rarely named. Grief for innocence, for stability, for the idea that things could improve if we just tried harder. Instead, the album presents a world where awareness does not equal agency. Knowing better doesn't stop the cycle. It just makes it louder.

In that sense, *Cool World* feels less like a protest album and more like a diagnosis. It doesn't offer solutions. It documents symptoms. Anxiety, rage, dissociation, dark humor, not as individual failings, but as rational responses to an irrational environment. The album understands that screaming into the void is still communication, even if no one is listening.

By the time the record ends, there's no sense of closure, only brute realism and cold questions. You don't leave feeling cleansed; you leave feeling touched by someone who has known you from the sidelines, which is arguably more unsettling. *Cool World* doesn't demand hope. It demands attention. It insists that noise can still carry meaning, that chaos can still be deliberate, that art can be ugly and precise at the same time.

Chat Pile has always treated sound as a weapon, a mirror, a wielded stabbing joke. With *Cool World*, they sharpen both. This is not music for escape. It's music for confrontation, with the systems around us, and with the parts of ourselves that have learned to survive in quicksand.

Lilly Goodyear is an Oregon-based writer, cinematographer, producer, and Co-Editor-in-Chief of alternative music publication, Steel Heart Magazine. Lilly loves listening to records on her floor when she isn't holding a camera or a pen. You can contact her at lilly@lillygoodyear.com.

Content Notes

An Influencer Asks A Very Sunburnt Middle-Aged Man How He Affords His Rolls-Royce Spectre by Kay Vaindal
- N/A

WireHead by Phoebe Sawchuk
- Suicide

Woman Parts by E.A. Harkins
- Body horror, medical gaslighting, blood, gore

The Oracle's Head by Kevin M. Folliard
- N/A

Play Me a Tune on Those Old Bones by Butch Farrell
- N/A

Puppet by Elizabeth Bottoni (AKA TechniGoth)
- N/A

The Unchanging by Jake Stein
- N/A

Look at These Poor Things by Carson Winter
- N/A

Reflections by Persee Tevebaugh
- Derealization

The Lyceum by Jonathan Louis Duckworth
- Implied/simulated incest, violence, graphic sexual content, mutilation

Meet the Staff

Sam Logan, Co-Founding Editor

Sam Logan (he/him) emerged in 1984 from the depths of the Chesapeake Bay off the Maryland shore. He made it to Oregon where he is a university professor in kinesiology and teaches courses about punk, body horror, and Taylor Swift. Sam lives with his partner, kiddo, and Dune the dog. He has stories in Mouthfeel Fiction, Punk Noir Magazine, Divinations Magazine, Major 7th Magazine, Creepy Pod, and Wallstrait, among others. His story "Belly Bees" earned 9th place in the 2024 TL;DR 2k terrors competition. Find him at samloganwrites.com.

Arwyn Sherman, Co-Founding Editor

Arwyn Sherman lives in the woods of Maine with a menagerie of animals including the ghost of a chronically ill ferret. Their work has appeared in anthologies, on a few stages, and is probably tucked away in a chapbook you forgot you bought at a late night poetry show. Their debut, We, the Missing, will be released in 2026 from Sobelo Books. For more of them, visit www.arwynsherman.com/

A.J. Van Belle is the illustrator of two children's textbooks published by J. Weston Walch. After receiving their bachelor's degree in art, they worked as a printing company's in-house illustrator. Their paintings and drawings have won awards and been exhibited internationally.

Born from the foggy oasis of the Pacific Northwest, Mike David was born with a pencil fused into his hand. As he got older, doctors surgically removed it, but he got used to the feeling and hasn't put it down since. Mike enjoys traditional art more than digital, so if you see any pencil lines underneath the line art, no you didn't. Mike currently resides in Corvallis, OR… for now…

Charlito Esposito is a forest creature inhabiting a cabin deep within a forest amidst a land rearranged by humans. *Rabidus. Inutilis. Nocumentum.*

Emma Fujikawa is an Oregon State University student majoring in graphic design. She hails from Kailua, Hawaii and became interested in art during quarantine. When she has free time, she also enjoys reading and playing casual soccer.

P.L. McMillan's short fiction has appeared in a variety of anthologies and magazines such as Cosmic Horror Monthly, Strange Lands Short Stories, Negative Space, and AHH! That's What I Call Horror, as well as adapted to audio forms for podcasts like NoSleep and Nocturnal Transmissions. In addition to her short stories, McMillan's debut collection, What Remains When The Stars Burn Out, and debut novella, Sisters of the Crimson Vine, are available now. Besides being a fiction writer, PLM has experience as an editor (Howls from the Dark Ages and The Darkness Beyond The Stars: An Anthology of Space Horror), hosts PLM Talks on Youtube (interviewing peers and professionals in the horror industry), and is the co-host of a horror writing craft podcast, Dead Languages Podcast. Find her at plmcmillan.com

SLUGGER

stories that hit you in the mouth

 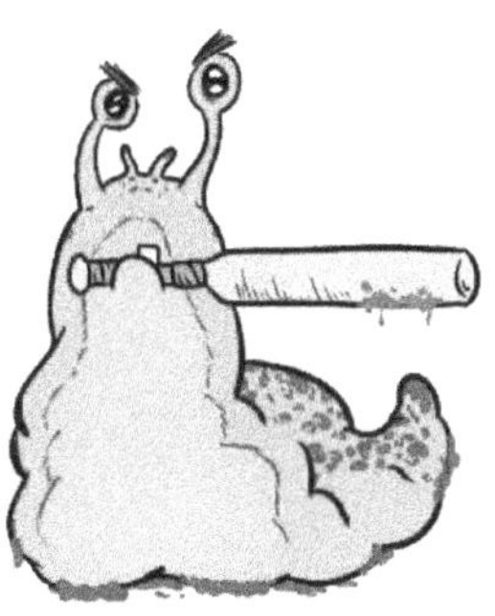

Enjoy the issue?! Consider a subscription.

www.ingramcontent.com/pod-product-compliance
Lightning Source LLC
Chambersburg PA
CBHW042049030726
47599CB00019B/2420